PRAISE FOR

THE TRANSMIGRATION OF BODIES

"Yuri Herrera's novels are like little lights in a vast darkness. I want to see whatever he shows me."

Stephen Sparks, Green Apple Books, San Francisco, CA.

"This is as noir should be, written with all the grit and grime of hard-boiled crime and all the literary merit we're beginning to expect from Herrera. Before the end he'll have you asking how, in the shadow of anonymity, do you differentiate between the guilty and the innocent?"

Tom Harris, Mr B's Emporium, Bath.

"Both hysterical and bleak, *The Transmigration of Bodies* builds an entire world in 100 pages. Herrera's ability to express everything in so few words, his skill of merging the argot of the streets with the poetry of life is unrivaled. The world his characters inhabit is dangerous and urban, like a postcard sent from the ends of the earth. Reading his compact novels is both exhilarating and unforgettable."

Mark Haber, Brazos Bookstore, Houston, TX.

"A fabulous book full of low-life characters struggling to get by. It's an everyday story of love, lust, disease and death. Indispensible."

Matthew Geden, Waterstones Cork, Ireland.

"Reading *The Transmigration of Bodies* was akin to being enveloped in a dream state, yet one that upon waking somehow makes profound sense. Another truly magnificent novel from one of the most exciting authors to emerge on the world stage for aeons."

Ray Mattinson, Blackwell's, Oxford.

"A microcosmic look at the lives of two families straight out of a Shakespearean drama. Pick it up and you won't put it down till you've finished."

Grace Waltemyer, Posman Books in Chelsea Market, NY.

"A work replete with the gritty, informal prose first displayed in *Signs* – rooted firmly in the modern world yet evoking the feel of an epic divorced from time . . . a cross between Cormac McCarthy and a detective novel, an incisive portrait evoking a Mexican *Inherent Vice*."

Marina Clementi, Seminary Co-op Bookstore, Chicago, IL.

"*The Transmigration of Bodies* reads like a fever dream: an intense, enthralling examination of how people live in a city of the dying and the dead. It takes an extraordinary amount of skill to combine elements of noir, political commentary, hardboiled crime, and allegory (not to mention Shakespeare, with a seasoning of existential ennui) and keep the novel moving, or in this case, racing along. Herrera, clearly, has at least that much talent, and then some."

Thomas Flynn, Volumes Bookcafe, Chicago, IL.

THE TRANSMIGRATION OF BODIES

Yuri Herrera

Translated by Lisa Dillman

LOS ANGELES · HIGH WYCOMBE

First published in English translation in 2016 by
And Other Stories
High Wycombe – Los Angeles
www.andotherstories.org

First published as *La Transmigración de los cuerpos* in
2013 by Editorial Periférica, Madrid, Spain

ISBN 9781908276728
eBook ISBN 9781908276735

Editor: Tara Tobler; typesetter: Tetragon, London; typefaces: Linotype Swift Neue and Verlag; cover design: Hannah Naughton; cover image (modified): iivangm; printer: Bang Printing, Brainerd, MN 56401.

A catalogue record for this book is available from the British Library.

This book has been selected to receive financial assistance from English PEN's PEN Translates! programme. English PEN exists to promote literature and our understanding of it, to uphold writers' freedoms around the world, to campaign against the persecution and imprisonment of writers for stating their views, and to promote the friendly co-operation of writers and the free exchange of ideas. www.englishpen.org

This book also was supported using public funding by Arts Council England.

For my mother, Irma Eugenia Gutiérrez Mejía

1

A scurvy thirst awoke him and he got up to get a glass of water, but the tap was dry and all that trickled out was a thin stream of dank air. Eyeing the third of mezcal on the table with venom, he got the feeling it was going to be an awful day. He had no way of knowing it already was, had been for hours, truly awful, much more awful than the private little inferno he'd built himself on booze. He decided to go out. He opened his door, was disconcerted not to see the scamper of la Ñora, who'd lived there since the days when the Big House was actually a Big House and not two floors of little houses – rooms for folks half-down on their luck – and then opened the front door and walked out. The second he took a step his back cricked to tell him something was off.

He knew he wasn't dreaming because his dreams were so unremarkable. If ever he managed to sleep several hours in a row, he dreamed, but his dreams were so lifelike they provided no rest: only small variations on his everyday undertakings and his everyday conversations and everyday fears. Occasionally his teeth fell out, but aside from that it was just everyday stuff. Nothing like this.

Buzzing: then a dense block of mosquitos tethering themselves to a puddle of water as tho attempting to lift it. There was no one, nothing, not a single voice, not one sound on an avenue that by that time should have been rammed with cars. Then he looked closer: the puddle began at the foot of a tree, like someone had leaned up against it to vomit. And what the mosquitos were sucking up wasn't water but blood.

And there was no wind. Afternoons it blew like a bitch so there should've at least been a light breeze, yet all he got was stagnation. Solid lethargy. Things felt much more present when they looked so abandoned.

He closed the door and stood there for a second not knowing what to do. He returned to his room and he stood there too, staring at the table and the bed. He sat on the bed. What worried him most was not knowing what to fear; he was used to fending off the unexpected, but even the unexpected had its limits; you could trust that when you opened the door every morning the world wouldn't be emptied of people. This, tho, was like falling asleep in an elevator and waking up with the doors open on a floor you never knew existed.

One thing at a time, he said to himself. First water. Then we'll figure out what the fuck. Water. He pricked up his nose and turned, attentive, to look around the place again and then said aloud Of course. He got up, went into the bathroom with a glass, pulled the lid off the tank and saw barely three fingers; he'd gotten up in the night to piss and the tank hadn't refilled after he flushed. He scraped the bottom with the glass but there was only enough for half. One drop of water was all that was left in his body and it had picked a precise place on his temple to bore its way out.

Fuckit, he said. Since when do I believe those bastards?

*

Four days ago their song and dance seemed like a hoax. Like the shock you feel when someone jumps out at you from behind a door and then says Relax, it's only me. Everyone was sure: if it was anything at all, it was no big shit. The disease came from a bug and the bug only hung around in squalid areas. You could swat the problem against the wall with a newspaper. Those too broke for a paper could use a shoe: no need to give them every little thing, after all. And *Too poor for shoes!* became the thing you spat at people who sneezed, coughed, swooned, or moaned *O*.

Only the ground floor of the Big House was actually inhabited, and of the inhabitants only the anemic student had actually been afraid. Once the warnings started he could be heard running to his door to spy through the peephole when anyone went in or out of the building. La Ñora certainly kept going out, keeping tabs on everyone on the block. And he'd seen Three Times Blonde go out one morning with her boyfriend. It unhinged him, having her so close, Three Times Blonde sleeping and waking and bathing only a wall and tiles away, Three Times Blonde pouring herself into itty-bitty sizes, her pantyline smiling at him as she walked off. She never noticed him at all, not even if they were leaving at the same time and he said Excuse me or You first or Please, except on one occasion when she was with her boyfriend and for a moment she'd not only turned to look at him but even smiled.

What did he expect, a man like him, who ruined suits the moment he put them on: no matter how nice they looked in shop windows, hanging off his bones they wrinkled in an instant, fell down, lost their grace. Ruined by the fetid stench of the courthouse. Or else his belongings just realized that his life was like a bus stop, useful for a moment but a place no one would stay for good. And she went for boyfriends like the one he'd seen – some slicked-back baby jack, four shirt buttons undone so everyone could see his gold virgin. The boyfriend had said hello, tho. Like the guy at the bar who tips on arrival so his drinks get poured with a heavy hand.

For the past four days the message had been Stay calm, everybody calm, this is not a big deal. On a bus, he himself had witnessed the pseudo-calm of skepticism: a street peddler had boarded the bus selling bottles of bubble gel; he blew into a plastic ring and little solar systems sailed down the aisle, oscillating, suspended, landing on people without bursting. Gel bubbles, he said, last far longer than soap bubbles, you can play with them, and he took a few between his fingers, jiggled, pressed, and puffed. One popped on a man's forehead. And just then the penny dropped: the bubble was full of air and spit from a stranger's mouth. A rictus of icy panic spread across the passengers' faces; the man got up and said Get the fuck off, the peddler stammered What's the problem, friend, no need to act like that, but the guy was already on him. When the guy lifted him up by his sweater the driver slowed – just a bit – and opened the doors so the vendor and his bottles could be tossed to the curb. Then he closed the doors and sped back up. And no one said a word. Not even him.

But at the time, they could still think they'd escaped the danger. Last night's news was no longer a dodge. The story had been picked up everywhere: two men in a restaurant, total strangers, started spitting blood almost simultaneously and collapsed over their tables. That was when the government came out and admitted: *We believe the epidemic* – and that was the first time they used the word – *may be a tad more aggressive than we'd initially thought, we believe it can only be transmitted by mosquitos* – EGYPTIAN mosquitos, they underscored – *tho there have been a couple of cases that appear to have been spread by other means, so while we are ruling out whatever we can rule out it's best to stop everything, tho really there's no cause for concern, we have the best and brightest tracking down whatever this is, and of course we have hospitals, too, but, just in case, you know, best to stay home and not kiss anybody or touch anybody and to cover your nose and your mouth and report any symptoms, but the main thing is Stay Calm.* Which, logically, was taken to mean Lock yourself up or this fucker will take you down, because we've unleashed some serious wrath.

He opened the Big House door again, took two steps out and was thrust back by the reek of abandonment on the street. Almost imperceptibly his frame flexed, anxious, updown updown, Fuckit fuckit fuckit, what do I do, and then he felt something brush his neck and he slapped his skin and looked at his hand, stained with insect blood. He stepped back, slammed the door and stood staring at his palm, transfixed.

What's going on? he heard behind him. He turned to see Three Times Blonde at the end of the hall. Half her body hanging out of her apartment, swinging from the jamb with one hand.

He took two steps toward her, wiping his hand on his pants.

What's that? she asked.

Grease.

Three Times Blonde relaxed a bit and asked again.

What's going on out there?

Nothing, he replied. And I mean not a thing.

She nodded. She'd probably been watching the news without daring to believe it.

Good morning, he said.

Afternoon, you mean, Three Times Blonde fired back. She blinked silently at the ground, an outburst held in, and then added I got no credit on my phone.

Take some of mine, he offered immediately, as tho gravity itself forced him to say such things in the presence of a woman.

Three Times Blonde stood aside, and tho they could have done the deal in the hall she ticked her head toward her place. Her apartment gloried in its own good taste: purple love seat, poster of a blonde on an armchair not unlike the love seat, blue rug. He asked if he *might possibly* have a glass of water, thinking she was the sort who put stock in proper talk, but she just shot him a strange look.

They trafficked his time and she turned her back to make her call.

Three Times Blonde's pants rode her all over. He ogled her like she was in a window display, seized by the urge to devour her, to gorge himself on her thighs and her back and her tongue and then ask for her bones in a little bag to go. He pulled her blue pants down slow and trembling – but no, he didn't lift a finger; he inhaled the nape of her neck and kissed the three-times-blonde hair on it – but no, his hands stayed folded before him like the tea-sipping innocent he knew he could pass for. She was on the phone saying So what's going to happen, are we going to die or what? Then why won't you come over? But you have a car, you don't have to see a soul . . . Oh. And there's nobody that can stay with them? Whatever. Well if you don't come now it's going to get worse and then you really will be stuck there forever with your mother and your sisters, yeah, yeah, I know, it'll all be over soon, fine, okay, yeah, love you too, kiss-kiss.

She turned back around. He's not coming.

He should have taken off right then, should have said You're welcome – tho she hadn't said thanks – and split. But his will wasn't his own.

Let's watch TV, she said, and went into her bedroom.

He approached, not daring to cross the threshold. The room was pink and pillowed. She sat on the edge of the bed and turned on the TV and patted the mattress. Come.

Suddenly he began to salivate, his mouth no longer a desert with buzzards circling his tongue but a choking street, a flooded sewer. He obeyed and instructed himself to move no further. The newscaster on TV was talking about the airborne monster, its body a shiny striped black bullet, six very long fuzzy legs humped over itself, and above the hump a little round head with antennae casting out into space and two tubular mouths. A bona fide sonofabitch, apparently.

Looks pretty determined, don't you think? she asked.

He nodded yes and swallowed spit, then said But who knows if that's even the one, maybe they just found a fall guy, maybe this bug's taking the rap for another bug's dirtywork.

It was a joke, but Three Times Blonde turned to him wide-eyed and said You are so right it's scary.

She was convinced. Maybe it was true, maybe he was right.

Then the power went out. Three Times Blonde's apartment, just like his, got no natural light since they were at the back of the Big House, so suddenly it was dead of night. She said Yikes! and then fell silent, they both fell silent, a sensual silence, surreptitious: no need to do a thing. No need for phony swagger and no need to shoot her sidelong glances as if the door were half-open, just sit tight, knowing she's within kissing distance, even if no one else knows it and even if you can't prove it, it's a leap of faith.

So that was what it felt like: not always thinking about the moment to come, wasting each moment thinking about the moment to come, always the coming moment. So that was what it felt like to incubate, to settle in with yourself and hope the light stays off. And astonishingly, like a miracle, she said: I think this is what we were like before we were babies, don't you? Little larvae, sitting quietly in the dark.

He said nothing. Her voice had brought him back to the mattress, there in her pillowed room. Again he wanted to touch her and again he lacked someone to loan him the will.

You want a drink?

Oooh, yeah, I could go for a vodka.

I got mezcal.

He pictured her twisting her lips.

Well. You got to try everything once, right?

They got up off the bed and she placed one hand on his arm and one on his back.

Don't fall. If you conk out I won't be able to pick you up. He let himself be led slower than necessary so she'd have to keep holding on. She opened the door and a square of light appeared from the small window in the door at the end of the hall.

Be right back.

He made it to the table in his apartment without fumbling, snatched up the bottle, and, with the skill of someone who's come home sloshed more than once, located the shot glasses. Before going back he walked to the end of the hall and looked out. He saw that the mosquitos had abandoned their puddle and what he'd thought was blood was in fact black floating scum. He recalled that on previous days he'd spotted several puddles covered in whitish membranes. This was the first black one he'd seen.

The city was still silent, overtaken by sinister insects.

On his way back he guided himself by the little inferno of her oven. The backlit blue silhouette of Three Times Blonde could be seen as she cut cheese, tomato and chipotle.

We're going to have something to eat, so I don't get silly when I drink.

They flipped and double-flipped and then folded the tortillas. Ate standing up. Then began to drink.

So how come nobody ever comes to visit you? she asked.

Everyone's fine right where they are, he replied. And me and mezcal don't talk shop.

Lonely people lose their minds, she said.

He always found it a miracle that anyone wanted his company. Women especially – men will cuddle a rock. When he first started getting laid he couldn't quite believe that the women in his bed weren't there by mistake. Sometimes he'd leave the room and then peer back in, and then peer in again, incredulous that a woman was actually lying there naked, waiting for him. As if. In time he found his thing: fly in like a fool to start, then turn on the silver tongue. Talk and cock, talk and cock, yessir. One time a girl confessed that Vicky, his friend the nurse, had given her a warning before she introduced them. Take one look and if you don't like what you see don't even say hi or you'll end up wanting to fuck. Best thing anyone ever said about him. It didn't matter that they never came back, or rarely. He didn't mind being disposable.

Three Times Blonde told him about her family. About a brother she never saw since he was a bad drunk and a hophead and when he was off his face he said awful things. About her mother, who introduced her to guys from work. Total scum. To illustrate what these people were like, honestly, she described their defining details: a lawyer from the office who would jam a napkin up his gums after eating and then put it back on the table, or this one guy who could never sit still and would readjust himself every other second saying, *I swear, my balls are just too damn big.*

Can you imagine? she asked. I mean these people. Honestly.

His type of people. Those were his kind, the kind he rubbed shoulders with, did deals with every day, the *nous* of his *entre nous*, his tribe.

Which is why it's so wondrous, he thought, why it's so weird, to be this close to her when we're from such different dirt. As Three Times Blonde spoke the whole house echoed in the absence of noise from outside, and for a minute he felt that now, really, all they had was time, and he got a good kind of creeps and was flooded with a patience he didn't know he possessed. But then she started talking about her boyfriend, as if he was different from all the others, If only you knew him. And using a new sound as an excuse he said Be right back, and went out into the hall.

He opened the door. There stood the anemic student, hunched, pale, dank hair dripping down his forehead like dirty bathwater. No doubt the guy hadn't ventured out in days and the smell of quesadillas had gotten to him. For a second he considered saying Come on in, compadre, fix you something right up. If he'd been another class of man or arrived at another class of time he would have, but all he said was Go home, you'll catch cold. He closed the door and went back to Three Times Blonde. Ha.

Three Times Blonde had put out a couple scented candles and was kicking it in the purple den. He poured her a second mezcal and they toasted, did it right, eyes on the shot glass – none of this staring into one another's eyes as if already wounded – and he downed it in one. Mezcal, so good so true. Distilled filth to filter his filth inside. He slammed the glass on the table and poured a third. Shots made him a better man: his teeth whitened, his wit quickened, his stiff hair stayed kempt and acted like it gave a shit. She didn't need it, of course, she was rosy-cheeked and graceful sans hoodwinkery, but she too downed hers in one. I always assumed mezcal was slimy since they make it with dead worms, she said. And him: No, the worm is what gives it life.

Like the nose on a u, she said.

Mmm?

You know how it has those two dots when it really sounds like u?

Dieresis.

The nose on a u. When it's with a q the u doesn't breathe, only when it's far from q, and it doesn't need a nose there. But I always put one on anyway.

She traced the letter in the air with one finger and dotted it. Like that.

He poured her one more and this time they did look into each other's eyes before down-the-hatching. She glistened like a wet street. This might be the last woman I'm ever with in my life, he said to himself. He said that every time because, like all men, he couldn't get enough, and because, like all men, he was convinced he deserved to get laid one more time before he died.

A flat silence slipped in from outside, the hours on the street withering in abandonment, while those in the house were watered in mezcal. But the mezcal was running low.

He had an emergency bottle at home. But what if the anemic student was there, curled up by the door waiting for them to toss him a tortilla. He was determined to hold out until the bastard had slunk back to his doghouse.

Sometimes I go outside in the middle of the night, said Three Times Blonde. If there's not much light you can see the stars. No way we can do that now.

He looked up a lot too, nights when he was still on the grind at dawn and the streets were deserted. But he kept that quiet, she'd never buy it.

So you were telling me about Prince Charming, he said; and she said Foo don't be mean.

He's very refined, she said. This is my first boyfriend, my first really real one.

Then she started saying she'd met him at a party, fighting to defend the honor of a girl being bothered by two drunks and she fell head over heels just like that; okay, she admitted, he's a bit cocky, and yeah he sometimes raises his voice, and sure he's insanely jealous and sometimes drinks a lot and fusses too much over Bronco –

Who's Bronco?

His car, silly.

He named his car?

Yeah, see he takes such good care of it. But when it's just the two of us alone together he is so sweet, if you could only see him.

Good grief. Little slickster, alias Angelface.

Something in the air swished a candle, flicking light onto Three Times Blonde's shoulder and suddenly he envisioned her unwrapped. Without thinking his hand reached out and very gently squeezed.

We went to the beach last week, she said, looking at him like he wasn't touching her.

With the other hand he turned her slightly and began, ever so softly, to squeeze more as her skin surrendered.

Mmm, that feels nice, she said. Keep doing that.

He kept doing it, inwardly faster and outwardly keener, with a tremble he fought by staring only at his next little crest of flesh. And then he began with his mouth. Just peeling off the wrapper and popping each little crest into his mouth. She cocked her head slightly to glance from the corner of her eye and said You are insane, you know that? He said Nnnf and kept at it.

When he got to her shoulder blade he came upon a scar like a line upturned at the ends, deep. He traced it with one finger.

How'd you get that?

My fucking deranged brother. When we were kids one day he lost his shit and tried to knife me with a spoon.

A spoon?

I'm telling you he's deranged.

He stopped touching the scar carefully, as tho afraid it might come off, and kissed it. She arched her back. He pulled down one spaghetti strap but before peeling off the rest traced his fingertips along the sierra of her spine. No longer leaning over to squeeze small folds of her, he slid across as if his arms were too short and he had to scoot right up to reach. As he kneaded another knot, almost to the edge of her back, he lowered the other hand to her hip and pulled her to him gently. For the first time she tensed.

You and me don't even know each other.

He stopped moving his hands but didn't take them off or release the pressure on her hip.

That's the best part, he said.

And even before he said what he said next, he could tell the bastard was back. Bastard alias the Romantic.

It's the best part, because affection is exactly what we need. Can you imagine what it would be like if instead of killing we cuddled? You seen how many people are out there hurting each other without even knowing who they're shooting at?

He believed that, he really did, and yet he was still a bastard because he'd said it like a man paying off the popo to disappear a ticket. Obviously he couldn't let this chance slip by. But still: bastard.

Three Times Blonde turned to look at him like he'd said something unforgivable. She stared tremulously a couple of seconds, then pulled him in by the neck and kissed him, sweeping her tongue across his as if surveying a new possession, marking more than kissing him, and he, already overexcited, had no idea what to do, but his left hand, which had twisted with her waist, and his right hand, which had landed on her belly, lent him the will that had wavered. He slipped his hands beneath her top and uncovered her breasts. They weren't like he'd imagined them, with his hands and his head, so many times: they're never the way you imagine them, they were smaller and pointier and one was slightly inverted as tho ordering him to suck it out, and as he obeyed he was shocked that Three Times Blonde started taking off his shirt, that she wanted it too.

He frenzied from breast to breast, undone by the inability to tongue them both at the same time. He licked his way down the almost-invisible trail of three-times-blonde peach fuzz that crept into her pants, which he unbuttoned, but before pulling them off he slipped a hand through her thong to finger her curls. He stood, fearful in that half-second she'd be overcome with ambivalence as he took off his own pants, but she was already stroking his stomach with the tip of one toe. He dropped everything but his unsexy underwear, knelt, and as he started to tug her panties aside heard Three Times Blonde ask What's my name?

He raised his head, racing breakneck through half-a-dozen idiotic replies.

Like you know mine.

That's not the same, you swine.

He'd had the good sense not to stop moving his fingers for the duration of that exchange and by the end Three Times Blonde had stopped worrying about names and he let his tongue revel the way a tongue can only revel when nobody's asking it for words. As soon as he sensed he didn't need further permission he pulled off her panties and got naked and pulled her to him by the hips but then she said Where's the condom?

Motherfuck the condom. He'd asked himself the same thing and had answered himself Don't fuckin worry about it right now.

He put his pants back on, said Don't move.

He stepped into the hall barefoot. The anemic student was nowhere to be seen.

He ran into his apartment reciting the prayer of the overheated horndog:

> *Oh please, oh please, oh please*
> *May he, the drunken me*
> *May he, the dumbfuck me*
> *May he, the me who never ever ever knows where shit is*
> *May he have saved one*
> *Just one*
> *Lubricated or corrugated*
> *Colored or flavored*

Magnum or tight-fit
Oh please
Holy Saint of horndogs
Grant me just one condom

But he knew there were none. He'd used that prayer the last time, months ago, and managed to unearth one under the bed, gleaming and glorious as a national hero. The very last one. This was not a time for heroes or miracles. Fear was what had granted him these hours of intimacy but now it was showing its virulent side. Go on, off to the shop, ladykiller.

Across the street was an old-school pharmacy run by little old men who still wrapped condoms and sanitary napkins in brown paper so the customer need not feel self-conscious on the way out, but in the mental photo he'd taken that morning the metal awning was down. He triangulated the hood in his head, locating shops and less-far pharmacies and said to himself, Be right back, no big deal. He walked out of his place and before walking back into Three Times Blonde's saw the anemic student at the end of the hall, staring at him, fiery-eyed, glassy, on his way out the door.

Three Times Blonde was still splayed across the love seat, transfixed by the shadows cast by the candle. He told her what he'd told himself:

Be right back, there's a pharmacy close by.

She sat straight up on the couch.

No no no, how could you leave with that thing out there, it's not like we're that desperate.

Evidently she knew nothing about him. In other circumstances he wouldn't have listened, but the current circumstance, the one that concerned him, wasn't the epidemic so much as Three Times Blonde herself, naked before him, adamant, insisting Come. That was all. No pharmacies and no condoms. Locked up with a woman who was calling him.

Like a wrestler, he said to himself, I surrender. He approached and attacked her tongue as he once more undressed and then she said We can't get comfy out here and led him into the bedroom where at first she just let him adore her unwrapped three-times-very-taut skin and run his lips across it and his fingers inside it, but then she put her mouth to his cock, no talk; they rolled around clutching bony and fleshy backs, round and skinny buttocks, until there in the center of it all he felt her so wet and so ready and so present that he just slid inside. It was worth it, no matter the price, just to feel her drawing his cock in from the deepest part of her body, even if only for an instant. He did it fast but in that time a million epidemics came and went, through a million deserted cities in which the only sounds were deep sighs, and then she, once more, looked at him like he'd done something unforgiveable, a thing that for one very long minute he did not want to end: she trapped him with the lips of her sex, with her legs, with her fingernails, and then said, in a steady but almost inaudible voice, Off.

He pulled out and slumped beside her. He thought she'd kick him out and told himself the same thing he'd told himself so many times in so many situations: All good things are but a part of something terrible. But instead of shouting at him she reached out a hand and took hold of his cock, squeezing and stroking steadily until he came, tho he begged Wait wait wait, stop, because he had his hopes set on who knows what.

*

He dreamed. Among the succession of images in his dream, a replay of his half-assed hungover day, was one of a black dog who turned up often; this time the black dog, shaggy and wet, was shaking himself energetically, whipping out shards of water like little sliced-up lakes, and with each sliver that flew off he felt himself – since the dog was also him – grow lighter, lighter, lighter, lighter, until he awoke so light he could touch the ceiling.

She was still there beside him. Not once in the night had he lost awareness that she was there. Not when he was an animal shooting out shards of water, not in the flickering light at the end of the hallway, not in the face of the anemic student staring at him one last time before he left, had he ever stopped knowing she was there, spooning him. Yet he told himself anyway: there they were, the two of them, at the same lock-in under the same roof.

He started stroking her from curve to curve. He heard the fridge start up behind the door and panicked. The power had come back on and he feared she might flip the lights and see him, squalid, ruining her mattress the way he ruined suits, so when he felt her start to stir he said Shh shh shh and slipped a gentle hand between her thighs to rouse her sex softly, awaken it gently. He moved his hand ever so lightly and as he did she moaned, and he moved a little more and felt his sorrow start to slip away and himself finally defeat what his roughneck cousins used to say to one another if they saw a drop-dead gorgeous girl: Ain't nothin the likes of you could do with the likes of that.

He felt her body contract and release and then languish again, but awake now.

Bet you can't do that, she said after a minute.

What?

See colors like I do. When I was a girl it was just bright lights but now I see colored lights.

What colors did you see just now?

I don't know. They were pastel. When they go out I forget.

This was exactly the way he wanted everything to stay. Let them bury me, he said to himself, let them scatter dirt on me, mouth wide open, snuggled up just like this. Let them bury me. Let them burn me and turn me, mark me and merk me. They can deep-six me if they want, but let everything stay like this.

Suddenly, like an involuntary twitch: guilt.

I meant what I said yesterday, he declared. I said it to sway you but I meant what I said.

She said nothing.

You mad?

That stuff about how great it'd be if the world was all loved up?

Yes.

Pfft, I knew that. What, you think I'm stupid? That's just a way to flirt, right? Why bring it up now? Silly.

Why indeed. She was right.

It's just habit, tricks of the trade, but I didn't want it to be like that with you. You know what I do?

Yes.

He sat up, and it was he who turned on the little bedside lamp to look at her.

You do? For real?

Of course. You're a fixer. Take care of stuff under the table at the courts.

He froze. For her to call him that, after all those kisses.

One time I heard la Ñora say The landlord told me not to bother the guy in 3 if he's late with the rent – that man knows a lot of people and he doesn't want any trouble.

He said nothing, but the silence was interrupted by his phone. He decided to answer. Like a man who goes to the john to sidestep the bill.

He picked up and said Yeah. No one spoke but he knew the half-lung wheezy sonofabitch on the other end of the line, and knew if he was calling now, with the city shut down the way it was, that he was needed and couldn't say no.

Who's this? the man asked, like he didn't know what number he'd just dialed.

Who do you think, replied the Redeemer. It's me.

2

Animals. They behave like animals, the Redeemer thought, watching a line of cats prowl the ledges along the block, and a small happy dogpack trot down the center of the street; they wagged their tails and cocked their ears, sneezed loudly, and when a car came along they parted with careful coordination before chasing it a few feet, barking at the tires. They're more clever when there's nothing in the way, he thought. The air seemed almost insubordinate with odors: because there was no smoke, the scent of jacaranda could be clearly discerned among the miasmas that had been blown uphill like never before, in the tropical storm that had skewiffed the wind like never before – and so the smells, rather than fading, fermented.

There were a few people out and about, but more like ephemeral grubs than lords of the land. A few in cars with the windows rolled up. In a park three blocks away, the man who used to predict the end of days, now alone, in silence, thrown off. A guy in a white robe crossing the street with quick steps. And pharmacies, two-bit pharmacies, open. The Redeemer stopped in one to buy facemasks and a bottle of water. The salesgirl served him from a disgusted distance and took his coins one by one through a handkerchief.

This doesn't seem so bad, the Redeemer thought, almost happy. Long as it doesn't last. And suddenly he no longer hated Dolphin quite so much for having hauled him from the bed of Three Times Blonde, who'd said Who in hell would order you out on a day like this? and pointed to the street. And he'd said An asshole with exceptional timing, and as she watched him get dressed she'd said You are seriously nuts, and then added: We were having fun, you and me, and now I'll have to lock the door when you come back knocking. The Redeemer had stopped buttoning his shirt a second to see if she meant it, and tho he could see that she did he'd kept doing up his buttons and said Don't know about you, but I make my living off the places people can't get out of.

Just then he hadn't wanted to get out of anything, particularly, yet his reflexes kicked in the second the phone rang and Dolphin said I need you to help me with a swap.

For who?

For me.

What happened?

Don't know. Shit went down last night. Someone took my son.

Romeo?

Yeah.

Of course he knew who had him, that was why he'd called. Not to locate the kid but to get him back. So who did Dolphin have? Who'd he want to exchange him for?

Where'd this go down? he asked.

Lover's Lane, said Dolphin.

The Bug eyed him with a distinct lack of urgency, as if to say You think I give a shit about epidemics? No car stares straight at you the way a Bug does, he thought. It was the most expressive thing on the block. The Redeemer got in and drove across the city to see what he could wheedle out of Óscar, a compadre of his who worked the bar at a cathouse. Lover's Lane was home to eight brothels in total, and together they tended to the various sectors of the population. There was one had cachet for kingpins and thugs with serious bank – even served champagne, and was staffed by girls who, word was, had appeared on soap operas. Two for those who liked to think they were street but lived nowhere near it, and tho those joints didn't splash out on pricey juice or fine females, at least they could keep the lights on. Four itty-bitty bordellos with classic red-light decor and cement floors for the roughnecks, who also had the right to kick back. And a big old tomcathouse for women who earned their own dough: disco ball on the ceiling, tiger-skin sofas, and strippers with huge muscles and tiny G-strings, ready to romp for the right price. Óscar worked at Metamorphosis, where the better-bred boys went once in a while to put hair on their chests. Next door was Incubus – the one for women – so Óscar always had hot tips on what was going down on Lover's Lane.

He found him standing at the entry, stroking his tash as he gazed down the empty street. The Redeemer was embarrassed to be wearing a mask and considered taking it off for a minute, but opted to leave it on.

How goes it, Óscar, my man?

It don't, Counselor, as you can see for yourself.

Óscar was one of the only people he could stand calling him that.

The Redeemer pokerfaced: You know the whereabouts of Romeo Fonseca?

Dolphin's boy?

Mhm.

Óscar had looked into the Redeemer's eyes and then stared down the street again, stroking his tash with a don't-know-jack face: obviously the Redeemer was about to ask him something and he was going to tell but it had to be clear he was not one to simply offer stuff up.

He was here last night, right?

Óscar nodded almost imperceptibly, like it was the natural extension of his tash-tugging.

He started off somewhere else – nodding now toward Incubus – then showed up here; after that I don't know.

The Redeemer let his true question ripen in the silence of the street.

Didn't see where but you saw who with.

Óscar finally took his hand off his face and pointed to a spot on the sidewalk, as tho conjuring the scene with his fingers.

Only thing I saw was him sprawled there. Couple kids came and put him in a van.

Kids, what kids?

The Castros.

The Castros, the Redeemer thought. Motherfuck.

How'd Dolphin find out?

You still on that prick's payroll? Óscar asked.

In his line, people fell all over themselves to say thanks if he fixed their situations, nearly wept with joy when he kept their hands clean of certain matters, they sent small checks and big bottles in gratitude. After that, tho, they didn't even want to say hey since it reminded them of what they'd been mixed up in. Maybe that was how he felt about Dolphin: just hearing the sound of that agonized wheeze reminded him of that one defining moment he tried to keep buried. But the Redeemer had never stopped repaying the man who'd stepped in to lend a hand at a rough time.

Still on it.

Mmm . . . well. Must've heard because his girl was here too.

The Redeemer eyed him, alarmed.

His daughter? The Unruly?

In the flesh. Up to her eyeballs she was, coming out of Incubus, saw it all go down but didn't say shit till after they took her sib, then screamed her head off, tho no one seemed to notice.

The Redeemer nodded. He pulled out the masks he had in his pocket, held on to one and handed the rest to Óscar.

These of any use to you?

Everything's of use to me here, he replied.

He drove back to his side of town, which was also where the Fonsecas were, some six blocks up the hill from the Big House. On the way he saw a train go by. Trains almost never went by anymore since they'd been sold off years back. But here was a convoy of eight sealed cars advancing slowly along the tracks. Carrying out the healthy or the sick? he wondered.

He parked in front of their big sheet-metal gate and slapped it ten times in a row so they'd hear him in the house, which stood beyond the slapdash patio that Dolphin had erected for parties. No one came. He beat on the gate ten more times and waited. Nada. He was about to start slapping again when he heard a bolt slide on the other side of the entryway.

Who's that? a girl's voice banged out. Her.

It's me, he said.

The Unruly said nothing, but the Redeemer could hear her breathing through the metal.

Your pops called.

The girl undid a second bolt and showed half an unfriendly face through the doorcrack – brow arched, nose wrinkled, mouth twisted. She said nothing. The Redeemer repeated Your pops called for me. Go ask him.

Don't you tell me what I can or can't do, spat the Unruly. She stared at him and then closed the door. After five minutes, she returned. Come back later, she said. Not right now.

The Redeemer snorted but didn't move, nor did the Unruly close the door.

Who'd you grab? he asked. Please not who he thought, please not who he thought.

The Unruly narrowed her eyes and said Baby Girl.

Shit. But that wasn't what he said. What he said was Where you got her?

The Unruly gave a sort of half-smile that said You must be kidding.

Why bother calling if you give me nothing to go on, he persisted, I'm not going to do anything, but I need to get an angle on this.

The Unruly pressed her face up to the half-open door. She smelled of brandy.

Real close. In that big white house. Cross from the elementary school.

Odd. The Redeemer prided himself on knowing about all the palmgreasing, hornswoggling, and machinating in the city, but this house had him stumped. Who owned Las Pericas? And why would Dolphin hide Baby Girl there?

Okay, he said, I'll be around, tell your pops to call me.

The Unruly slammed the door, and he listened to her walk away.

He got a text from the government assuring him that everything would be back to normal any minute now, that it was essential to exercise extreme caution but not to panic: a reassuring little pat on the head to say Any silence is purely coincidental, okay? Like when people are talking and everyone goes quiet, like when an angel passes, like that. But it came off more like Better to play down than stir up.

Baby Girl. The Redeemer recalled the first time he'd met Baby Girl on a job he did for her dad: itty-bitty thing, quiet, long hair always carefully brushed, pretty face but eyes so sad. The kind of girl you wanted to love, really truly, but then the urge passed kind of fast. Even for her family. The Redeemer had seen it, at a big blowout after that job, seen the way they treated her like a piece of furniture from another era, one you hold onto even tho it's uncomfortable. The Castros had been putting on airs for years and Baby Girl cramped their style. Now the Fonsecas, too, had struck it rich, but about style they couldn't care less. So different and so the same, the Castros and the Fonsecas. Poor as dirt a couple decades ago, now too big for their boots, and neither had moved out of the barrio: they just added locks and doors and stories and a shit-ton of cement to their houses, one with more tile than the other. So different and so the same. If he thought about it, in all these years he'd never once seen them cross each other. Until now. Odd for them to butt heads right when there was finally enough room.

But he'd seen this before, the way old grudges resurface. Even in this city, where people didn't nose around, no matter what was done or who was doing it, sometimes it could almost seem like We're all one. Don't matter if your thing's a burning bush, some lusty dove, a buried book, big bank, talk or cock, there's room for us all. But no sir, he knew better, the real deal was: Don't give a shit what you're doing but you better not look at me, fucker. Every once in a while people did look; every once in a while they remembered what they'd seen. But man, for this all to go down now – just when everyone and their mother was cowering under the bed?

He passed by the local park once more. The grass on the median looked overgrown tho it had only been ignored a couple of days. Inside the park, in a little fountain where a colony of frogs used to live, he saw none; the water was dead, bereft of ripples; for a second he considered bending down to drink from it because he'd only bought one bottle and finished it, but opted instead to walk another block to the pharmacy.

The pharmacy was closed. On the metal shutter a piece of paper: *Out of Masks.*

He'd been told, that time, to go get Baby Girl from some corner store in a barrio stuck on the side of the hill. A boyfriend had tried to abduct her, but at a traffic light she got out of the car and ran into the shop. The boyfriend followed but when he tried to drag her out, the owners chased him off and someone called one of Baby Girl's brothers – yes, everyone knows fucking everyone. Before the brothers could head out to butcher the boyfriend, tho, their father stopped them, calling in the Redeemer to keep it from escalating into a major shitstorm. The boyfriend wasn't on juice, or blow, or smack, he just couldn't stand Baby Girl getting feisty and refusing to go with him when he'd made up his mind. The Redeemer got to the corner store, made sure Baby Girl was okay, and she was – pallor and little-lamb panting were as much a part of her as eye-color – then went to sweet-talk lover boy.

Hey, hey, amigo, listen up a minute. I got no dog in this fight, okay, I just want to say one thing and I'll be on my way. Cool? Listen, man, I'm with you, I know what it's like – respect, that's what it's all about, and it's your girl those lowlifes got socked away in there, not theirs, right? Thing is, tho, people don't see you been disrespected if you don't make a fuss. Times it's better to let things slide and come off like a king, comprende? All I'm sayin, a badass ain't the one to raise his voice but the one with no need to – just think on it. And the boyfriend not only thought on it but thanked him and heartily shook his hand before shouting into the store: But we ain't through, Baby! And sure enough, two weeks later they were back together. That was no longer his problem. The Redeemer sweet-talked only as much as he had to. Let people get in all the tight spots they want; he'd be out of a job if he started passing judgment on their vices. That same night, when he took Baby Girl home, each time he asked her what the boyfriend had done, she said Nothing, señor, honest, I just didn't want to go with him.

He helped the man who let himself be helped. Often, people were really just waiting for someone to talk them down, offer a way out of the fight. That was why when he talked sweet he really worked his word. The word is ergonomic, he said. You just have to know how to shape it to each person. One time this little gaggle of teenage boys had gone to the neighbor's on the other side of the street and stoned the windows and kicked the door for a full half-hour, shouting Come on out, mother-fucker, we'll crack your skull, and the pigs hadn't deigned to appear; that was one of the first times the Redeemer had done his job. He went out, asked in surprise how it was they'd yet to bust down the door and added You want, I'll bring you out a pickax right now, and that sure calmed them down; see, it's one thing to front, to act like a big thing, but burning bridges, well that's a whole 'nother thing. Soon as he saw what was what the Redeemer added: Tho, really, why even bother, right? Man's in there shitting himself right now, and they all laughed and they all left. That was when the Redeemer learned that his talent lay not so much in being brutal as in knowing what kind of courage every fix requires. Being humble and letting others think the sweet words he spoke were in fact their own. It worked on others but not on him. He'd met politicians who could believe whatever came out of their mouths as long as others believed it too. He tried to learn how but could never forget lies. Especially his own.

He trusted Dolphin – or trusted him as much as anyone who'd been a buzzman for twenty-five years can be trusted – but the Las Pericas thing was prickling his neckhairs. What was up with that? He decided to ask Gustavo, a sharp-witted lawyer who knew the ropes and had been untying the city's secrets for decades. He called, but a woman's voice said he wasn't in and who knew when he'd be back.

He needed someone to watch his back. He called the Neeyanderthal and climbed back in the Bug to go get him.

The Neeyanderthal was an entrepreneur of sorts: it was all bidness for the Neeyanderthal. Everywhere you look, he liked to say, looks like wheels and deals. He bought old cell phones that he sold at new prices to credulous clients, organized office pools at places he didn't work, and shuffled the cash flow to keep all his balls in the air: he smuggled shit in, sold intel, rented his house out as a place for petty crimes to go down. He never had any money. Instead his rackets seemed designed to prove he was cleverer than everyone else, to bring him doses of euphoria followed by stretches of contained rage. The Neeyanderthal was huge and hulking, a man who walked like he was forever on his way out of the ICU, moving each muscle with considerable care.

Years ago the Neeyanderthal's brother had died in his arms, on the way back from a nearby town: some kid had crossed the road in front of them, the Neeyanderthal jammed on the brakes, the brother flew through the windshield, the truck flipped and by the time the Neeyanderthal could get out from under it, his baby brother was dying on the white line and kept right on dying even as the Neeyanderthal held his face, sobbing into it saying Hold on, man, almost there little brother, as tho that could extend his life. It didn't. Finally the ambulance came to pick up the body, by then so lulled and soothed it looked almost at peace.

To the Redeemer it seemed the Neeyanderthal had been trying to off himself on blow for years. After the brother thing he launched into more honest attempts. Provoking police, street fighting. Then one time while he was truly looped he came right out and tried to shoot himself through the heart. Like it was no big deal, people were at his place getting trashed, and he got up, went to his room and fired a shot. His luck was so bad one of the credit cards he kept in his pocket to cut coke deflected the bullet, which flew up, barely kissed the top of his heart and came out his back. They found him standing unsteadily with a lost look on his face. Guess this ain't a boneyard kind of day, he said, and claimed he was smiling when he said it.

The Redeemer had never contemplated suicide, not even the time Dolphin had pulled him out of that black hole. Whenever he heard about someone who'd decided to cut their own life short he was shocked, especially if it was someone who had the strength to defend themselves; it surprised him not because he thought it was wrong but because he suddenly saw that person like they belonged to an entirely different species, and was astonished they inhabited the same planet. People who could make decisions they weren't prepared for. So you want to inhale ammonia? You fuckin sure? Dead silence.

He got to the Neeyanderthal's place, rang the bell and went back to the Bug to wait.

He watched a junkman pull his cart up the middle of the street. The junkman looked at the Redeemer in his mask, smiled with superiority, began hacking dramatically, then shook his head side to side and kept on his way.

The door opened.

What's up, Neeyan? asked the Redeemer.

Damn, man, not a tail to chase or a soul in sight, said the Neeyanderthal, staring out the Bug's window at the empty streets.

The Redeemer crossed an avenue with two military trucks down it and turned in another direction.

First time there's no traffic and I still got to take the long way, he said.

At the next avenue they caught sight of a very small funeral procession: one hearse with two cars following behind, three people in the first car, only one in the last.

Oh, yeah, said the Neeyanderthal, looks like people are real choked up over this fuckin corpse.

Passing the procession the Neeyanderthal stuck his head out and said aloud, as if addressing the body in the hearse, You're fooling yourself, man, you're fooling yourself.

He would say that about anything: a political argument, a lover's secret, a soccer game. Afterward he'd add something smartass; in this case, once his head was back inside the Bug, he said Should've vacuum-packed your ass . . .

Dependable as gravity, that was the Neeyanderthal. He messed with everyone like it was an obligation. Why was he the Neeyanderthal's compadre? Was it because they'd once been real friends? Was it that he'd watched him grow sadder and sadder? Or that in him he saw something of his own black dog? That's why we make enemies of our friends as soon as they start to drift, he thought, cos that way they get stuck with all our flaws, unlike when they're shared. Maybe brief friendships are best. If you pull out in time, the vices are all theirs.

Close to his barrio the Redeemer turned and found himself head-on with another military truck. This time he couldn't dodge it so he braked slowly and started a U-turn but a soldier waved him to where he should stop. He parked the Bug and waited. The soldier approached the car, peered into the back seat, then at the Redeemer and finally at the Neeyanderthal, who said What? I didn't hear anything about a curfew. Can't a man go out anymore without catching shit?

The soldier walked around to the Neeyanderthal's side and stared at him with no expression, making no attempt to bend down. Then he glanced back to the truck and nodded toward the Bug. A masked officer approached and ordered the Redeemer out with an index finger. He got out. Another soldier was patting down a punk rocker, palms against the truck.

Good morning, Captain, the Redeemer said.

The captain's eyebrows arched almost imperceptibly, seeming to indicate an appreciation for the Redeemer's knowledge of rank. But what he said was: Afternoon, you mean.

The captain stared at him as tho chewing a twig. Patient, reflective. The Redeemer realized he'd do well to keep quiet and silently composed his best body language to say: You say jump, Captain, I'll ask how high. The captain glanced sidelong at the Neeyanderthal and said Couple of smartasses, I see.

The Redeemer half-closed his eyes in apology.

Captain, I can't even imagine what you must have to put up with in a situation like this, the thing is, sir, we're all uneasy, as you can imagine, and the only thing we really want is to get home and lock ourselves up.

At the truck, one of the soldiers had pushed the punk against the hood and spat The fuck is all this crap you got on?, slapping his ears, his lip, where he wore rings. The boy accepted the slaps without raising his hands.

Going to have to take you in and do background checks, the captain said.

But suddenly he'd stopped looking at the Redeemer: he turned his attention to the soldiers by the truck and said Take that shit off him. One of the soldiers cuffed the kid's hands behind him and the other began to rip out the rings. The punk writhed in silence, trails of blood starting to run from his eyebrows, his nose, his mouth. The Redeemer sensed this was his chance to dig a hole in the wall and sneak out. Another day he'd have tried to help the kid, but today it was a no-go.

Any chance you could do me a favor, officer? I certainly don't want to take up any more of your time.

He took out one of the business cards that boasted a degree he'd never earned and said In case I can ever be of any service to you.

The captain took the card but didn't turn to look at it. He waited a couple seconds, then with his left index finger sent him back to the Bug, and with his right ordered the soldiers to put the punk in the truck. Thank you, Captain, the Redeemer said. He got into the car and started the engine.

They drove several blocks in silence and then the Neeyanderthal said Dude was asking for it, right? You walk around like a faggot, all that metal in your face, you pay the price.

And the Redeemer replied Shut up.

Go to Las Pericas, said the text from a number he didn't know, but it could only have been Dolphin.

With some people it was hard to take the measure of their mettle till you saw them in a very tight squeeze. With Dolphin there wasn't much mystery. Ex-buzzman, divorced, one son and one daughter. He'd earned his nickname when he burned a hole in his nose snorting too much blow; as if that wasn't enough, he then got shot in the chest and could now only breathe through one lung. Even so he managed to act like these were still the days when he wore a tin star, carried chrome, slapped people around on the street. Still: the Redeemer wasn't expecting to hear him say what he said when he went to see Baby Girl.

He got to Las Pericas with the Neeyanderthal, and the Unruly was already waiting outside.

Only one goes in, she said as soon as she saw the Neeyanderthal, and tell this guy to put on a mask or get the fuck out of here.

The Redeemer handed Neeyan a mask, which he used to wipe his mouth, like it was a napkin, and then threw on the ground. The Unruly's little eyes shone like she was smiling.

Go on in, she said to the Redeemer.

The Las Pericas place was huge and white with a big wooden veranda, as if someone had been unwilling to give up their old house in the tropics, despite now living on a hill a thousand klicks from the sea. This was the first time the Redeemer had ever been inside. As soon as he stepped through the door he was dazzled by a huge room with a dozen high windows. In the center stood a table, and on the table lay Baby Girl.

He didn't need to get close to know Baby Girl was no longer all there, but still he had to do it, and to look after what was left. He approached reluctantly, his steps slow, as tho in place of bones he had a barbed-wire soul. He saw Baby Girl there, pale, ashen, a trail of blood between her nose and mouth, hands clenched and face exceedingly sad. She was so small and so still, but at the same time seemed like the heart of the house, cold yet somehow keeping it alive. Who knew how many dead bodies he'd seen, but this one reminded him too much of the other one, his one.

That was when Dolphin appeared behind the Redeemer, and said – there in the brightest room in the world, pointing to the loneliest girl in existence – I still got it. They try to fuck me over? I still got it.

This job would be easy if the only ones we had to fight were our friends, the Redeemer used to say, but what he said to himself now was I don't want to listen to this motherfucker, and

I do not even want to think about the eye-for-an-eye bullshit, the tooth-for-a-toothery this is going to unleash. On other occasions he'd convinced himself that even the most twisted men deserve a chance, since people, all people, are like dark stars: what we see is different from the thing itself, which has already disappeared, already changed, even a single second after the light or evil has been discharged. But this . . .

What did you do to her?

Nothing new, said Dolphin.

Why here? Why you got her here?

Not your concern, asshole, said the Dolphin patting his head, not your concern. You seen her, now get to work.

The Redeemer felt in his gut the desire to wrench off what nose Dolphin had left but the rest of his body couldn't carry out the order. He turned and walked out of the house. Outside, the Neeyanderthal was talking to the Unruly.

So, what line are you in, sweetness?

The Unruly was on the verge of saying something different but when she saw the Redeemer her look hardened and she said, Revenge.

The Redeemer held her gaze and contained the urge to take her by the shoulders and shake her. He ought to have done it, ought to have beat Dolphin till not his nose but his whole face was destroyed, if he wanted to salvage any vestige of himself. Behind his back he heard Dolphin approach laboriously and say Don't pay her any mind. This ain't about getting revenge, just about getting even.

3

What do you mean am I sure? Vicky retorted after the Redeemer asked if she'd go with him. Shit, you've already been out on the street with the Neeyanderthal, right? But did you ask him if he was sure he wanted to go? No. Right, asshole? Dumbass can't shoot for shit, can't hit himself with his own damn gun, and there you are dragging him all over town, but me, who takes care of every fucking thing under the sun for a living, I'm some little señorita that needs your protection.

He couldn't help it, it wasn't an attempt at gallantry, just came with the job: in the Kingdom of the Word all men were Chiefs and all women Lil' Ladies, as far as he was concerned, and tho he was well aware that Vicky was not only nail-hard by nature but also an adrenaline junkie, he couldn't help but lil-lady-fy her. On occasion Vicky helped him out with dust-ups, taking things down a notch, smiling, acting wise – which she was, always – and sweet, which she was, sometimes. On occasion, like now, she helped him get a read on a body.

I need you to do it fast, he told Vicky when she climbed into the Bug in her nurse's uniform. But do it good. I need to know if she was beaten.

The Neeyanderthal started shaking with laughter, stomach only. They both gaped at him.

The fuck did you have for breakfast, man? asked the Redeemer.

It's just, that's what I tell the ladies too: Gonna do you fast, but good.

No one else laughed. Seeing Vicky's look of hatred, the Neeyanderthal tried to put things right: Oh, hey, sorry bout the trucker mouth. It just slipped out.

If only you really were a trucker, Neeyan, Vicky said. But you're not, you're just tedious. The most tedious people in the world can't take anything seriously. Don't worry tho – and with this Vicky patted the Neeyanderthal's cheek – don't worry, I speak Hombre, so I know you're not actively trying to be a prick, you just have no control over your little bullshit organ.

The Redeemer didn't know if the Neeyanderthal and Vicky truly hated each other or simply had their own brand of love. He remembered something that had happened just after the brother's death. They'd been out boozing and he heard the Neeyanderthal recount the accident to a woman, the whole damn thing – stupid pedestrian, flipped truck, death throes – as a line. Neeyan didn't actually want to open up to the woman, but he recited the drama in an attempt to open up her blouse. The Redeemer had said to Vicky that that was low, even for the Neeyanderthal, but she put on a sad that's-not-the-whole-story face and said What do you expect, Neeyan cuts a profit whenever he can, and right now all he's got is his scar. If there was a market for it, he'd cultivate kidney stones and piss them out. Leave him be.

Before returning to Las Pericas they made a stop at Vicky's ex-boyfriend's parents' place. Actually he was an ex-lover, one Vicky loved for real, but his time was up and she hadn't backed down over the ultimatum. Vicky might be willing to suffer but suffering wasn't marital status, and his marriage was already on public record.

They're in a state of total hysteria, she said, packed in like sardines because the alarm went off while he was over there with his wife. Dropped in to pay back some money he owed and now they don't want to leave . . . seems someone's sick, and he convinced them to let me stop in and have a look.

He: the ex-lover. Vicky's face softened a bit at the mention.

Can I go with you? the Redeemer asked. Might be able to get something from the father – the nouveau always have the lowdown on each other's riche. Maybe he's been cooped up so long he's ready to wag his tongue. Plus he knows me, I've worked with guys close to him.

Vicky took out a pair of latex gloves and handed them to the Redeemer.

Don't touch anyone.

They rang the bell. A clipped argument could be heard coming from within. Go; No, let him go; Fine, I'll go; No, don't you go, mother; Oh, let her go; No, I'll go.

Ha, Vicky snorted. Their servant split so it looks like they'll have to learn how to turn a doorknob on their own.

It was He who answered. No mask. He smiled poignantly. A smile that said I'll always love you but my promises are in the pawnshop. He was a sad, handsome little devil. He looked at the Redeemer like an electrician who'd come when the lights weren't broken.

He's with me, Vicky said, and he knows your father.

They were all in a living room full of wood-and-red-velvet furniture – nostalgia for a finer form of pretense. An antique apiece and a drink apiece. The mother in the armchair, vodka on the rocks in hand, sloshed; the perverse twenty-year-old little brother at one end of the sofa, whisky on the rocks in hand, sloshed; the father in a high-back armchair, brandy and coke in hand, episcopally sloshed. You could sort of see that they were scared, but could more clearly see their ennui. We never know how much we actually hate one another, the Redeemer thought, until we're locked in a room together.

Which one's the patient? Vicky asked, eyeing the range of red-faced tremble-handed possibilities.

The ex-lover pointed to a door:

Her.

Vicky shot him a profoundly scornful stare, nodded and went to open the door. At the back of the room, sitting on a bed, a woman in a blue dress sat holding a teacup. She was wearing makeup but it couldn't hide the sneer of someone who swallowed bile every day as tho it were water. Vicky observed her from the doorway, the Redeemer from the living room. She took two steps in, put her hands on her hips, observed the woman a little longer, turned and closed the door.

There's nothing wrong with her.

You didn't even examine her, he said.

Stop rationing her booze, that's what she needs.

The silence that ensued would have been awkward in any other room, but in that one each member of the family merely clutched their drink a little tighter before sinking back into a slight stupor. The Redeemer sensed this was his moment. He approached the father and crouched down.

Remember me?

The man made an effort to wrestle his way out from the bottom of the bottle, finally found his pupils and focused on the Redeemer.

You once got some photos back for a friend of mine.

The Redeemer smiled.

Exactly. I'm dealing with something less serious now, but I need some information. You know who the Las Pericas house belongs to? Place no one's lived for years?

The man seesawed behind his eyeballs, forward and back, as he thought it out. Except for a hand faintly jiggling his ice, the rest of his body was still.

The Fonsecas, he said. Tied up in some legal mess, I think, but far as I know, it's theirs.

Yes, it's theirs, the mother interrupted from the depths of her vodka, for as much good as it does them.

Thassaway it is with those sorts of families. Now it was the perverse baby brother who spoke in a whiskified slur. Don't matter how many houses they buy, they only know how to live in crappy-ass shacks.

The Redeemer felt his fist wanting to bust the kid's nose, in part for that remark, but more because he wanted to bust the monster's nose regardless. This was the first time he'd seen him in the flesh, tho he knew what a class act this little shit was. He and some other silverspoon whose family had a funeral home had been caught snapping shots of each other with the bodies they were supposed to prepare: posing as if kissing or slapping the corpses, drawing moustaches on the dead, sticking hats on them. Then some other kid they'd showed the photos to started telling people and it was about to blow into a big scandal when the Redeemer stepped in and disappeared the pics. The funeral home kid got a slap on the wrist; the little shit, not even that.

One more thing, Vicky said to the whole family. In case this is spread by mosquitos I'd recommend you stop wearing perfume; they're attracted to it.

No one said a word, nor did anyone except the ex-lover make a move to stand when Vicky and the Redeemer headed for the door, but Vicky put up a hand in front of his face and said That's far enough.

Back in the car, the Neeyanderthal said Bet they offered you a drink in there – and me out here like a dumbfuck.

On the way to Las Pericas the Redeemer saw a corner flower-stand peeking out above the hunkered-down city and thought of Baby Girl, alone, injured, growing cold in that house, no one to talk to her. He stopped, said Wait for me, got out, and bought flowers. There were no Day-of-the-Dead marigolds but they had gillyflowers. Now that he thought about it, that stand never seemed to close, even on holidays or the darkest nights.

They arrived and the Redeemer got out to speak to the Unruly, but she didn't need convincing because she'd seen who-knows-what in Vicky's authoritative eyes, so all Vicky had to say was Don't worry, I'll be right back.

She even reached out to tuck a strand of hair back behind the Unruly's ear and tho she didn't smile, she didn't flinch either.

They stayed in the car and smoked while Vicky worked. The Unruly smoked, too, leaning up against the doorjamb. They finished one cigarette. Lit a second. Finished the second and lit a third and that was when she came out. Vicky gave the Unruly a pat on the back, which morphed into some sort of sororal squeeze; she leaned in a little more and whispered to her. Then headed for the car.

What'd you just say? asked the Neeyanderthal.

That we women need to look out for each other. No one else is going to do it for us.

What did she die of? asked the Redeemer.

This shit. Vicky waved vaguely at the world outside the car. But she must have gone days without treatment to die like that. By the way she held her hands you can tell she couldn't stand the pain in her joints, and from the blood in her mouth and nose it's clear the symptoms advanced to late-stage with no meds.

So was that why they had her locked up?

She hasn't been dead long, but that girl was sick for days before they got to her.

Did they do anything to her . . . after she died?

Vicky stared straight ahead a few seconds without saying a word. She looked tired.

They didn't fuck her, if that's what you're asking, but they did something. That shitbag Dolphin put her underwear on inside out.

He had no idea who from but knew at some point a message would arrive. And when it finally did, he realized right away who was running the show on the other side of the corpse.

What's up, Friend? Meet you on the corner over by Casa Castro.

There was only one person who called him Friend with a capital F: the Mennonite.

The two of them had met on a job they worked together, in a place a long way away from the place the Mennonite called home. They were going to pick up a body. The deceased was a family friend, which was why when the Redeemer arrived he found the man attempting to stitch up a finger.

No way am I handing him over like this, as if he was off to just anywhere.

The Mennonite was standing on the corner like a tree that had sprouted out of the sidewalk. These days he no longer wore the denim overalls and straw hat but the workboots and plaid shirt were still there. His red beard spilled out the sides of his facemask.

They hugged and the Redeemer asked:

So. What brings you way over here? You never used to leave your land.

Well, you know. Unhappy people aren't the problem. It's people taking their unhappy out on you.

I do know. Yeah.

The Mennonite had left the land of his kith and kin on his own, and had adapted to the world of those always in a rush – silence and simple toil replaced by engines and cement. But at least back there he'd had his people nearby. Now, not even that. Who knows whose toes he must have stepped on, why he had to strike out on another path. Still. It was time to get on with it.

What's the story? he gestured toward the Castro place.

Boy's in there, the Mennonite responded. They didn't touch him.

I'm going to have to ask him that myself.

Fraid that's going be a bitch, Friend.

The twist in the Mennonite's lips filled the gaps left by his words. There was no longer a Romeo to ask.

Fuckit, said the Redeemer. Same story on this side.

He tried to explain in a way that made it seem he understood more than he did: the Fonsecas hadn't killed Baby Girl, she'd died of the disease, and all the body needed was to be prettied up a bit.

The Mennonite nodded and took a deep breath and then said This is the truly fucked-up part. Wait for me here. He turned and walked back to the Castro house.

In the two minutes that went by before Baby Girl's father came out, it felt like the street contracted and began to throb. The Redeemer took out a smoke then thought better of it and put it back in the pack, glanced at the Castros' place and then turned the other way. He crossed his arms. Fuckit, he repeated.

He heard the Castros' metal door open then slam shut, and then panting, encumbered by sobbing, and steps approaching. He shot a quick sidelong look at the Bug and with an almost-imperceptible hand-pat signaled Stay put to Vicky and the Neeyanderthal.

When he felt him a half-step away, the Redeemer turned to face the man. Tho they knew each other, Baby Girl's father stared and stared and stared without recognizing him, and steadily with each passing second the man aged as the news inhabited his body, despite his attempt to resist it, his attempt to hold it at bay with rage. He slammed the Redeemer against the hood of the Bug and started shouting in his face.

Bring her to me! You bring her to me now! In one piece, you sonofabitch! You bring her to me safe and sound, right now!

The man was clenching his fists and trembling and still making up his mind whether to throttle the Redeemer. Then his boys flew out of the house, berserk. The older one wielded a club and the younger one a bat, itching to find something to justify their tunnel vision, their hatred. As soon as he saw them, the Neeyanderthal got out of the Bug, thumbs hooked through his beltloops; Vicky stepped out too, slower, eyeing them from her side of the car. One of the two must have made an impression on the brothers, who continued their approach, but slower now. The younger pointed his bat in the Redeemer's face.

The Mennonite held a hand up and said That's not the way, son.

The kid stared at the Redeemer, reluctant to let go of his rage, but then his father began to sob and both boys dropped their weapons to the ground and held him.

The Redeemer thought they'd do better to scratch the wound than bandage it: those who lose a child shouldn't be consoled; parents die to make room for their kids, not the other way around. He wasn't being cruel; he just felt that a gash that deep had to be respected, not swaddled over with cuddles.

Sir, said the Mennonite, Will you let the nurse-lady in? Just for a minute.

The man nodded without looking up.

We're going in too, the Neeyanderthal said.

The man nodded again. Okay let's go, he said, turning toward the metal door and heading off, eight hundred years older than when he'd come out it the other way.

In the Castros' living room hung a family coat of arms. The Castros had been noblemen and lords in some century or other in some castle or other on the opposite side of the world – and there was the colorful coat of arms to prove it. They were different from the Fonsecas that way: the only things the Castros held on to from their poorer days were those they'd marshaled up from many generations back. On the walls of the Castros' living room, besides the coat of arms, there was nothing but photos of the boys in team uniforms and a diploma granted to Baby Girl for having finished her degree in psychology. Psychology. For fuck's sake.

They descended a freezing staircase. The basement was full of shadows cast by a dim corner lamp backlighting a dozen chains with hooks from which hung calves, turkeys, and half a cow. The Redeemer didn't say a word but at the sight of his raised brows, Castro said We don't trust outside meat.

In a room adjacent to their private abattoir he saw Romeo, laid out atop some boxes. One of his legs was falling off the side, as tho he'd made a quick move to get up. They encircled the body in silence. Only the Neeyanderthal rubbed his hands together, saying Damn it's cold. Vicky approached and began to study what was once Romeo. The Redeemer noticed he was dirty, that he still reeked of alcohol and had marks on his knuckles but no sign of blows to the face. Vicky examined his head and opened his shirt and palpated his ribs, sunken, beneath a blue bruise. The Redeemer turned to the Castro kids, whose hands were in their pockets.

What went down, muchachos?

The Castro kids were spitting images of their father, differing only by the quantity of hair on their heads and the way their flesh fought what was going on inside each of them. The older one jerked his shoulders up and down in a childish gesture and said We didn't do jack. I mean, we talked shit earlier on, but we didn't fight.

We liked him, said the younger one, sneaking a look at his father and continuing. Our jefe here always says the Fonsecas are fuckin users and climbers, but the son was a good kid.

So what'd you say? This was on Lover's Lane, right?

Mhm, said the older one. We saw him on our way into Metamorphosis, and since he was going somewhere else we thought he was headed for the swanky strip club, so my bro here said Hey, pretty boy, this ain't Vegas you know, and he said Fuckin deadbeats, I come here cos I carry big bills, not loose change. Stuff like that.

But we were just smacktalking, said the younger one. Even if it sounds like we wanted to fight.

There's some people you just mess with, that's just the way it is, said the older one.

The Redeemer nodded. He knew what they meant.

Then what?

That was early, the older one said. We took off after a little while to hit the other clubs, and we were on our way when we saw Romeo again, he was pretty looped, in the parking lot – no idea where he was going but he was staggering back and forth – and that was when he got hit by a van. It was backing up and I don't think they even saw him.

The Redeemer stiffened in shock but didn't dare turn and look at Vicky to corroborate what they were saying.

A van? You're telling me a vehicle did this to him?

S'right. Tapped him and took off. Me and my bro here went to see if he was okay. He wasn't breathing good but said not to call an ambulance, said it would pass. We picked him up and put him in the back seat of my car. Then we took off too, but on the way he asked us not to take him to the hospital, said please just let him hang with us a while, lay low and then he'd go home.

The Redeemer walked over to stare at the boys, straight into their eyes – back, forth, one, the other – searching for signs of a leaky lie.

And you didn't lay a hand on him. That was it. You're sure.

The boys nodded.

Well, said the older one, not all of it. We brought him back here and we were going to call a doctor but when we got him into the house he suddenly got real real light, and then heavy, and it took us a few minutes to realize he'd died since we didn't think he was doing that bad.

Here? Kid was sick and you brought him down here?

No, upstairs, we were in the living room. But then someone called.

A girl, the younger one piped in.

Yeah, a girl, and she said the Fonsecas had Baby Girl and weren't giving her back till we brought them Romeo. Which is why we didn't call and brought him down here instead, so he wouldn't rot.

The Redeemer turned to Romeo, whose hands Vicky was now examining. Romeo looked rough, but like his rough had come from earlier stuff and not from dying, as if the only thing dying had done was ashen up his skin, but you could tell there was prior pain.

Give us a minute, the Redeemer said, not turning to anyone in particular, and the Castros left the room.

By the way, the Mennonite said. Someone's out to jack you up. Boyfriend of one of your neighbors. Watch your ass, amigo.

Fuckit, how did little beau slick get word? And how did the Mennonite, who wasn't even from around here, know about it?

You giving me a tip-off or a warning? he asked.

Both, but not cos anybody told me to. Little punk's got no balls of his own and was looking for a hardcase to rough you up. Guy I know got asked and I'm just passing it along, free of charge.

The Redeemer shrugged no-big-thing shoulders and asked So, what about this?

The Mennonite crossed his arms and eyed Romeo.

I think they're telling the truth.

Not entirely, said Vicky. I buy the story about the truck but that doesn't explain his hands.

Oh, the Mennonite said. That was me.

The other two stared.

He looked a little too tidy to have died in a brawl.

He didn't die in a brawl.

But his father isn't going to believe that, is he? Why make matters worse by saying they didn't lay a hand on him? Those two families got bad blood between them. So let them believe what they want to believe, let them bury their boy like a hero. They're not going to simmer down when someone tells them to, they'll do it when they're worn out. So tell them what happened, but let him look like he had a fight first.

Vicky looked as if she was about to say something but thought better of it. And then she said: Why wouldn't he want to be taken to hospital?

Now that part I can't explain, the Mennonite replied.

They walked out and Romeo remained alone once more. They went upstairs to the Castros and before they left the mother appeared, frightened and pale, and demanded Now tell me what they did to my little girl.

The Redeemer decided the Mennonite's strategy wouldn't wash with her and said: More or less the same as what happened here. A tragedy with no one to blame.

What are you saying? That she's dead? That each of us ended up with the other's body by accident? Is that what you're telling me?

Something like that, yes.

The mother stared straight at him and said Those things just don't happen.

Some sad fuck so much as takes a bite of bread and we got to find a name for it, he thought. Or an alias anyway. That's about as close to the mark as we get.

Banished man alias Mennonite. Broken man alias Redeemer. Lonely old soul alias Light of my life. Ravaged woman alias Wonder where she's gone. Get revenge alias Get even. Truly fucked alias Not to worry. Contempt alias Nobody remembers him. Scared shitless alias Didn't see a thing. Scared shitless alias Doing just fine. Some sad fuck alias Chip off the old block. Just what I was hoping for alias You won't get away with this. Housebroken words alias Nothing but truth.

I got to buy condoms, the Redeemer remembered aloud.

Vicky eyed him mockingly.

What, your hands are too calloused?

No. From time to time there occurs a miracle.

Vicky gaped as if to say You got to be kidding – you, talking miracles? But Vicky didn't get it. Vicky was beautiful and a hardass and used to striding across a room and grabbing any man she wanted by the balls and dragging him into her bed without losing her head or getting quixotic. She'd never had to work to find someone to fuck, and he pitied her that a bit, just as he pitied those who don't know what it feels like to see a big city for the first time because they grew up in it, or the guy who can't recall what it is to feel handsome for the first time, or to kiss someone who seemed impossible to kiss for the first time. Vicky knows nothing of miracles.

Yeah, sometimes the ladies let their guard down, right? the Neeyanderthal said.

Oh god, said Vicky.

Here we go, she's going to tell me off.

No, I'm not, it's just that you don't get it. At all. See, men will fuck a chair, even if it's missing a leg, but when women fuck an ugly man or a jerk it's not because we'll fuck any old thing, it's cos that's the way things start and we know there's more to it. Men don't come to see that till years later, once they've stopped mounting anything that crosses their path.

Thanks, sweetheart, I knew one of these days you'd come to appreciate us.

This only applies to men with a soul, Neeyan.

So maybe Vicky simply understood different things. Either way, the Redeemer braked and left the two of them there in their silence when he caught sight of a pharmacy. He got out of the car but immediately saw it was closed, and the metal shutters had been beaten repeatedly with a pipe or a club or a desperate fist, and beside the shutter hung a penciled sign reading *No facemasks*.

Dammit. Oh well, he had work to do. Maybe he'd find somewhere open on the way. He returned to the Bug and rolled down the window so as not to hear the silence between Vicky and Neeyan, but the silence of the street slipped in instead: a stubble field of frantic signals emitted from the antennae that fear had planted in people's heads. He could sense the agitation from behind their closed doors but sensed no urgent need to get out. It was terrifying how readily everyone had accepted enclosure.

He drove back to the Castro house, didn't stop, circled the block twice and headed for Las Pericas. He had to see where he'd hit a checkpoint, which he would: no such thing as a free ride, no matter how hard you hope. A block before Las Pericas they came upon another funeral procession. Normally he'd have passed it, to avoid waiting out the whole mournful motorcade, but this was the saddest cortege he'd ever seen: in the hearse no one but the chauffeur, and behind the hearse one lone Bug with a single person inside, facemasked.

He circled the block Las Pericas was on then headed to the Neeyanderthal's, assessing the street all the while. One would think he'd find fewer obstacles than ever, but the fear seeping from beneath people's doors threw him off his game; he stopped at every corner to look both ways, glanced in the rearview every twenty seconds, and each time he did he saw the same thing: asphalt about to rear up at him. Things had been roiling in the background for some time, but now you could see the bubbles starting to rise.

He dropped the Neeyanderthal at his place and the man got out without a goodbye for anyone. Next he headed for Vicky's. They passed the funeral procession once more, stopped now at a checkpoint. One soldier was opening the coffin and two more interrogated the chauffeur and lone mourner.

Assholes, said Vicky. As if the corpse is armed.

They passed one more pharmacy, also closed, with a sign in the window: *Closed for funeral.* He dropped Vicky at her place and made for his own. Perhaps he should do the swap there, given how riled up both families were. When he got back he saw that on the house next door someone had written on the wall *Clean up you pigs that's why we're in this shit.* And sure enough, there was a black puddle running from the front door to the gate, tho no insects hovered over it. He looked up. In truth there was nothing to see but a wall of tepid clouds blocking the stars.

He walked into the Big House. Standing a moment at one end of the hall he debated which of the four doors to head for: the anemic student's, to smack him around for being a shitstirrer; Three Times Blonde's, where he'd fall to his knees and beg Please please please, for the love of all good things, wait for me just a little longer; his own, to see what was going on; or la Ñora's, to sound her out about the body swap. Bingo.

He knocked. He heard no steps but la Ñora opened almost immediately, without looking through the peephole. She eyed the Redeemer with an odd intensity, trying to place him or perhaps keep him at bay. She said not a word.

Good afternoon, señora, said the Redeemer.

Evening, you mean, la Ñora replied automatically, tho it seemed like her mouth hadn't moved.

Right, yes, evening. Ahh, listen, señora, I just wanted to let you know I'll be having some people over tomorrow. Not for long – they'll just deliver something and go – but there will be several of them.

La Ñora stared, no change to her inscrutable expression.

I wanted to let you know so you don't worry, in case you hear anything.

You're going to have people over, la Ñora said. And you want me to keep my nose out of it.

Sharp lady, la Ñora.

The Redeemer smiled. Just don't want to worry you, señora.

La Ñora gave a nod. The Redeemer, too, nodded good night and turned. As he was about to enter his place la Ñora said Sir, then faltered. Young man, she tried again: have you seen the boy?

Answer me but keep your nose out of it, she said with her eyes. On the surface she looked the same as always, fierce and wary, but the Redeemer saw, now, a certain tender tremble and almost wanted to embrace her. He'd keep his nose out of it, tho. The anemic student. Who'd have thought.

No, he said. But I'll let you know if I do.

La Ñora nodded again and closed the door. The Redeemer stood a few seconds struggling with mental images of la Ñora and the anemic student, ate a two-day-old sweet roll and went to knock on Three Times Blonde's door. He heard her body stylizing its steps and saw the light behind the peephole go dark. They both stood breathing silently but the door didn't budge. Finally Three Times Blonde said Have you been wearing that facemask all day?

Yes, the Redeemer lied.

Three Times Blonde waited another minute and opened up slow. She took a step back, and the Redeemer walked in and shut the door. The moment he did, he cornered Three Times Blonde, pulled down his facemask and began to kiss her. She let him, arms at her sides, body limp but tongue responsive. In that single second the Redeemer thought of all the people who'd breathed in his face that day and the bug he'd smashed on his neck and the who-knows-what already coursing through his veins, yet here he was, a brazen bastard overexcited at the miracle of breasts and diereses before him. What a sonofabitch. Maybe she could sense the Redeemer's black dog pawing at her chest. Maybe she simply wanted to know. Either way Three Times Blonde pushed him aside.

So who you been talking to?

Lots of people.

Who you been talking to about me, you swine? she asked, and on stressing the *me* scratched the Redeemer's arm with a long red nail.

Not a soul. Why?

After you left my baby came over all keyed up wanting to yell at me, asking who'd I let in my house and I don't know what-all.

That wasn't me. That was the damn neighbor.

Three Times Blonde looked unsurprised.

I know.

So why ask?

Because men always talk. It's like they have to report everything to their friends. Jerks.

Ouch. Three Times Blonde had taken a shot in the dark and hit him right between the eyes. And called the other asshole baby.

He left without even saying goodbye, she continued, looking mournful. The Redeemer stroked her cheek.

You feeling sad? he asked, suave.

No.

Three Times Blonde slid her hand under his shirt and stroked his chest, then suddenly slid it down into his pants and squeezed his cock, palming his balls, weighing them.

The condoms, she said.

The Redeemer pulled her in by the back of the neck and began to kiss her. She tried to pull away and oh did he not want that to happen, please no, and in his head he attempted to shoo the bugs and people and shuttered pharmacies, but inevitably Three Times Blonde pulled his arm off her and scooted aside and said Pull . . . out . . . a . . . condom.

The Redeemer donned a now-where-did-I-put-it? face and for a second fostered hopeless fantasies of finding an open drugstore, but before he could lie again, Three Times Blonde said You didn't buy any. Stupidass neighbor. You didn't buy any.

She did stick-em-up hands, as tho she couldn't even bear to brush up against the Redeemer, opened the door, and said I got shit to do.

He begged and pleaded for a moment with his eyes and with her eyes she told him to go fuck himself, and so he went, pitiful and utterly dejected, and let the slam of the door push him home.

He walked in and threw himself down on the bed.

Some nights, when the black dog left, he imagined sleeping curled up inside some other animal, protected from the cold. But that night the black dog stayed.

4

In the faint light of his fitful sleep he saw Óscar's outstretched hand, pointing, and suddenly sat up in bed because he knew somehow it contained a clue to how this grimreapery had begun. He called the Mennonite, explained what he was thinking and they agreed to meet on Lover's Lane. Back to the Bug he went, back to streets buzzing behind closed doors, back to zigzagging around corners rife with aimed rifles, rife with thugs both uniformed and civilian. When he arrived the Mennonite was already waiting at the entrance to Metamorphosis. There were lights all down the lane and cars outside the cathouses but no one wandering from one to the next. They walked into Metamorphosis and he scanned the bodies below in search of Óscar.

The place was packed, placid but packed. There were people asleep underneath tables and asleep on top of tables – like really sleeping, not booze-induced sleeping. And those who were awake were conversing with the dancers. Normally they paid little attention, as if women taking off their clothes before a gaggle of drunkaneers was totally unremarkable; now they sat, chatting, nobody drooling, nobody tail-shaking. One lonely soak at the bar slurred It's aaaaaaaall over, It's aaaaaaaall over, again and again and again. Everyone else was cool and attentive, as if listening to hailstones on a tin roof.

They haven't been out for days, he heard Óscar say behind him. Claim it's too dangerous but you ask me, this is their chance of a lifetime.

I see you made use of those facemasks, the Redeemer said. One girl was dancing before a cluster of liquored-up fools, naked but for the mask over her mouth; each time she leaned close she made as if to take it off, and the boozers whooped in titillation.

Fuck yeah, said Óscar.

Óscar, the Redeemer said. The Fonseca kid. You sure bout where you saw him come out of?

Óscar glanced at him for a single second: long enough to draw up, read through, sign and notarize a confidentiality clause between the two of them.

Girls' place, yeah, he said. He was referring not to these girls, the working girls, but to the customers.

Appreciate it, brother.

They left Metamorphosis and entered Incubus. The clientele was less numerous but more boisterous, only a dozen or so women, rorty and sloshed. They sat at the tables with two or three strippers, drinking. The floor was empty.

The Mennonite addressed the madam, a stout elegant woman with very black hair.

I'm looking for a boy.

Hm. We generally cater to a female clientele but it's always possible to arrange something.

The Mennonite cast a glance around the tomcathouse, studying the handful of men, and said: I'm looking for one with a steady boyfriend.

The madam observed them distrustfully. Then she got it.

Must be that one, and she pointed to a young man, almost a teenager really, attempting to smile at the woman buying him drinks. He's been acting all mopey. Must've had a fight with his boyfriend; guy used to come pick him up after work but I didn't see him last night.

They approached the table where he sat. The Redeemer bent over the woman the kid was hooking until he was almost brushing her cheek.

Let me borrow him for one sec, amiga, just a quick word and then he's all yours.

She batted her eyes diplomatically and the Mennonite nodded the boy over to the next table.

I don't sleep with men, he said as soon as they sat down.

We know, said the Mennonite. Or rather, you only sleep with one.

The Mennonite spat the words, resting his hands on the table as if he might backhand the boy at any moment. The kid suddenly looked scared. The Redeemer's approach was more gentle.

Tell us what happened two nights ago.

He came in. We argued about the same thing as always – and with this he gestured, taking in the whole of the whorehouse with one hand – then he took off. Didn't even wait for his sister.

His sister. Fuckit.

Did they come together?

Yeah, but he ran off and it took her a minute to follow. It was crowded that night. And then neither of them came back.

They rose, intending to leave, but the boy stopped the Redeemer with an arm. What is it, what happened to him?

Get some sleep, the Redeemer said. But tell them to give you the day off tomorrow. By then we'll know for sure.

They walked out and the Redeemer lit a cigarette and stood smoking by the Bug. It was time to call Dolphin. He dialed.

I got bad news, he said.

Dolphin was silent, or his mouth was anyway; the lung wheezed.

Romeo's dead, he said. But the Castros aren't to blame.

He listened to Dolphin wheeze down the line and then hang up with no reply.

He was tired of delivering that kind of news, and now he felt bad for not having delivered it to the one person who may have truly cared. Motherfuckit.

He got a very few hours of straggly shuteye, alternating between simple dreams of tires in motion and cats on ledges, and got up with neither vigor nor languor. Please let it be a dull day and not some deranged vigil.

He tried Gustavo again, the know-it-all legal beagle. Not home. Letting himself be guided by an early morning urge he got back in the Bug and drove around behind the Big House for a tamale sandwich; only at the empty corner did he remember there was no one out on the streets. He was hungry as hell. And thirsty. But all there was was rankystank water in a few puddles on the path and those dense gray clouds that refused to squeeze out a drop. A synthetic insanity to the weather, the city, the people, all sulking, all plotting who-knows-what.

He headed for Las Pericas. Suddenly he saw something in the middle of the street and slammed on the brakes. A huge heap of rags, or hacked-up dogs. He dodged the pile and eyed it as he passed: it was neither of those things; it was a man, black with sludge. The Redeemer thought he looked familiar. He rolled down the window and stuck his head out. It was the junkman he'd come across the day before, mouth stuffed full of facemasks, eyes wide as an illuminati. The Redeemer rolled up the window, rolled on.

Before ringing the bell at Las Pericas he pulled the facemask out of his pocket. It was stiff with too much spit on one side, too much world on the other; what good was that now? He put it back in his pocket and rang the bell.

The Unruly poked her head out a window, then opened the door and stood to one side. The Redeemer walked in and saw they'd put several bags of ice on Baby Girl, whole unopened bags. Despite all the ice it was as if you could see new life there, see some color, sense something new inhabiting her. He pulled off the bags and tossed them aside. Then he tried to lift her, but she was so heavy. He looked at the Unruly, maybe she'd agree to help, she seemed softer, more compliant than before; but in the end he decided to carry the body by himself. We're going to be all right, he said to the shell of Baby Girl as he hoisted her up in his arms and headed out into the leaden morning.

The Unruly, without his asking, walked alongside, opened the Bug's door and even shifted the passenger seat up so he could place her inside. Her body wasn't yet stiff, so he was able to arrange it as tho Baby Girl had curled up for a siesta on a road trip, raising her head from time to time to ask Are we there yet, are we there yet?

What's this? Where to? asked the Redeemer as he watched the Unruly get in as well.

I'm coming with you.

Didn't they tell you how this works? Me and another guy like me make sure everything's okay, and then – and only then – do we make the switch.

Right. But they also told me to see where you put her. It's not like you're the one running the show.

He started the car. No sooner had he turned the corner than he saw a couple kids take off running, something in their arms. He had a hunch what it was about and pulled up. Indeed, someone had broken the lock on a corner store and they were looting the place bit by bit. Lowlifes. Still, he stopped the car, got out, grabbed a few bottles of water and two prepackaged sandwiches, and left a few bills on a high shelf in the hopes that the kids wouldn't be able to reach them. He was wolfing down the sandwiches before he'd even left the store.

There were even fewer cars out now. On one avenue, where trying to cross normally meant taking your life in your hands, the only thing on the street was the fear of penned-up people. As if everyone's prejudices about everyone else had suddenly been confirmed.

They say some people are spreading it on purpose, the Unruly announced, as tho they'd both been thinking the same thing.

He didn't reply but did turn to look at her. He glanced at her hands: fleshy and soft, a yellowy stain at her fingertips. With all the facemasks he now looked more at eyes and hands. If this carried on, people would end up IDing one another by their fingernails.

I met your brother-in-law, he announced abruptly. The Unruly turned to him, little-girl fear on her face.

That's right, the Redeemer said. You going to tell me what happened?

The Unruly stared straight ahead and crossed her hands, struggling for self-possession. The Redeemer decided to push a little harder.

Romeo. The Castros didn't touch him, did they.

The Unruly shook her head slowly side to side.

No. When I went outside he was already on the ground and they were just going to him.

And why didn't you go to him too?

Now it was her turn to stare at her hands or perhaps out past her hands.

The Redeemer was about to ask something else but she said: He didn't like for people to see him sad, down. I don't know if that was why – because he'd have hated me for seeing him like that – or if I was too drunk to understand what was going on. I'm drunk almost all the time.

This girl would cry if she had any fucking idea how, thought the Redeemer, seeing the way she let her eyes fall to the floor, utterly defeated. And then the Unruly did cry, cried short and hard, without changing her expression, maybe without realizing she was crying.

He didn't want to go out, he really didn't, she repeated. He was scared of this shit. The sick people, all those dirtbags coughing up blood. He didn't even like going to the doctor, he was that scared of places with so many fucking sick people.

So why'd you snatch Baby Girl?

My father said to, told us to take one of the Castros, said this time they were going to pay, is what he said. So I went out because I'd seen Baby Girl hanging around here before and she was always alone. When I found her she was leaving home, on her way out, and she looked bad; I told her to come with me and she didn't even ask why or where to. When I got her home my father was so happy, and then we put her in the car and took her to Las Pericas. That's when I saw she had blood coming out her mouth. We put her to bed but she didn't last long after that.

But didn't you ask Dolphin why he was doing it?

I did, but all he said was: Be loyal to your family, do as I say. So I said I'm sure Romeo isn't that bad off. I don't know if he really believed me or whatever it is he has against the Castros just became more important, but the only thing he said was: He's my son, I'll handle it how I see fit.

The things people inscribe on tombstones, even if only with their breath. I will love you always. I can never forgive you. Forget about me. I'll be back. You'll pay for this. Words that etch deeper than a chisel. Erasing those things was what the Redeemer was there for. He excelled at nothing but the ability to diminish malediction; to free folks from cell blocks, or their own promises. The fact that he was never in the way meant he could be used like a screwdriver and then stuck back in the toolbox, no need to thank him at all. That fix you're in? Take care of it *entre nous*. That secret of yours? We'll keep it *entre nous*. That fine you got? *Entre nous*, let's lower it; that alibi you need, *entre nous* we'll cook it up. Dirtywork is providence.

That was what he knew, how to efface set-in-stone truths. But he still had nothing to grab hold of in this tale of lonely deaths, nothing but pieces of lies. Solid lies, but lies nonetheless.

In the rearview he saw a black truck riding up on them hard, several yards behind. He slowed to let them pass but the truck pulled alongside, someone in it looked at Baby Girl and then it cut them off. Two badasses emerged with faces that confirmed they were indeed very big badasses. The one who got out on the passenger side didn't have to tell the Redeemer to hustle. The Redeemer turned off the engine and got out. The badasses weren't wearing facemasks either.

Girl gets out too, said one of them.

The city had seen other times when people died by the cartload, but back then it was bankrolled black lung and mass mine collapses – the usual. Perhaps because life was short, people had learned not to stick their noses into the affairs of others: existence was already a bitch without worrying about them as well. Perhaps that was also why they were all so fixated on form, on nicedaying and areyouwelling and thankgodding and tookinding. Mechanisms to mark distance. But these thugs knew nothing of etiquette.

The Unruly got out of the car and went and stood behind the Redeemer, arms crossed.

What'd you do to the other girl? asked one.

Nothing, she died of this shit.

The badass adjusted his dark glasses, took a few steps toward the Bug, stared at Baby Girl a few seconds and returned.

You need the body?

I do, said the Redeemer. Only reason I'm out is so I can deliver it.

Thing is, we need a body, the badass said. But I guess there's lots of them around these days.

He said something to the other badass and they got back in their vehicle. The Redeemer and the Unruly returned to theirs.

Normally it's the dead that are rotten, not the living, the Unruly said.

Her proclamation made the Redeemer want to up and forget about everything and have everybody up and forget about him. He wanted to crawl under a rock or onto some furniture. Who knows why we were left here like collateral, he thought. I guess some other Redeemer will negotiate our release.

They arrived at the Big House and he handed the Unruly the keys to start clearing the way, got Baby Girl inside, lay her on his bed. The Unruly stared at the Redeemer's possessions as tho shocked to see he didn't live in a cave, then said I'm outta here, don't move her without telling us.

And she left.

The Redeemer leaned back against the wooden table by the bed and tried to look Baby Girl over with a professional eye, but it was hard since what he really wanted was to sit and hold her hand. So that was what he did. She was cold but still a little soft.

We'll get you cleaned up, young lady, he said.

He stood, smoothed her skirt, closed her eyelids all the way, combed her eyebrows. He found an iron he hadn't used in months, carefully removed Baby Girl's cardigan and ironed it on the table and then put it back on.

What else? He knew there was more but he had no desire to do those things and didn't know how. He'd ask Vicky to help. He pulled out his cell: no signal.

He went out to the street, arranged to go pick up Vicky, then called the Neeyanderthal. Get over here, it's almost time.

The Redeemer was about to go back into the Big House when he saw Three Times Blonde turn the corner. He stood waiting for her at the entrance and, when she arrived, gestured with his hands to say Huh?

Three Times Blonde tossed her head and said Seeing as you're so useless . . .

She took him by the hand and pulled him indoors. She walked in front, smiling at him – this time most definitely at him – with her little pantyline.

Before going into her place the Redeemer said Let me lock up.

Like you have treasure in there, she said, not knowing that today more than any other day he would have happily stabbed someone to protect what was inside.

He turned the key in his lock and went to Three Times Blonde's place; she took him to her room and pointed to the bed. Lie down.

The Redeemer lay down and in the time it took him to wriggle out of his clothes she'd taken off all hers. That was the first time he'd seen every bit of her, a burning miracle of flesh. He thought he might come just from staring at her waxed lips, her landing strip; that he might come in the anticipation of sucking her breasts, which looked larger and more obliging than last time; that he might come just from envisioning the feel of her ass in his hands and the way he'd lay her down on the bed and this time, yes, o thank you most holy saint of horndogs, finally they would fuck; and he tried to get up but she said No: I said lie down!

He lay down and watched Three Times Blonde touch herself with both hands; then she knelt on the bed and slid him into her mouth.

The Redeemer clutched at the sides of the mattress as she ran her mouth and hands over his cock. He wanted to say Stop, but never ever ever ever would he tell her to stop, and just in time she pulled him out and said There. She opened the little box of condoms she'd placed on the dresser and as she took one out the Redeemer said Weren't you scared of going out on the street?

What scares me is the stupid shit people are doing on the street. Not being there.

And she put the condom on him.

Don't do a thing, she said.

She knelt over the Redeemer and began very slowly to lower herself down so that he entered her. He could feel his cock changing temperature as it made its way inside. Three Times Blonde began moving in circles, moving almost without moving, from the inside out. Then she let herself fall over him, brushing his chest with her nipples, and slipped her tongue into his mouth, and he ran his hands down her back and held her hips, which never stopped grinding. Everything was better. She was better, life was better, this woman wetting herself with his cock – nothing better could possibly occur in the rest of his everloving life. He made no attempt to show her what he could have done, and she fucked him at her own sweet speed, all by herself, until she straightened back up and came as if her bones were going to burst through her skin, arms back, stuttering one single vowel with each spasm. Then she fell back on top of him and he rocked her hips with his hands, and she continued to come in little splinters, in quick intakes of breath, until he too was done.

What colors did you see? he asked.

Black, she said.

He heard noise outside. His other instincts activated immediately; he moved Three Times Blonde gently, got up, put on pants and shirt, and left.

Dolphin was inside the Big House. He was bent over the Redeemer's door trying to work the lock with a credit card. By his side, the Unruly looked on anxiously.

What's wrong, Chief? the Redeemer asked.

Dolphin turned, looked the Redeemer over from head to bare feet, and said You didn't tell me you were bringing her over here already. Didn't even give me a chance to leave her a little token of appreciation. You go on back to whatever you're up to, don't mind me.

Fraid you can't do that, Chief.

Dolphin straightened up with difficulty and gazed into the Redeemer's eyes.

Trust me, kid, I got your back.

And lightly palmed his cheek several times, pat pat pat.

The Redeemer sensed his black dog there behind the door, silent, hulking, like the very first time he appeared, when Dolphin had said exactly the same thing, years back.

He wasn't the Redeemer back then; back then he was nothing but a brickshitting ambulance-chaser carving out a career in fifth-rate courts.

Some buzzmen had stopped by the pen to beat the everloving life out of a man who was already all bloodied up, a mess of a man kicked more times than he could take. Don't let him get away, they'd said on their way out, as if the man could do anything but cower in a corner and swell up.

The man was fading in and out and on one of the ins stared back with his single working and seriously crapkicked eye. It was an empty stare, pure light in a pure state, until he managed to force all his strength into it and said something, his pupil dilating. Help me, or Don't leave me alone, or Touch me, or Release me. He approached the man, who made slow mysterious gesticulations in the air. What, what, what do you want me to do? The man kept his good eye glued on him, and it slowly shrank smaller and smaller then opened wide one last time along with his one last breath and he couldn't even take the man's hand, so he crouched down before his face, not voicing a word but with his eyes saying Hold on, hold on, we'll work it out.

A few minutes later the buzzmen were back, and wordlessly one grabbed the man by the armpits and the other by the ankles and they began to lift. That was when the Redeemer came to life and, in an authoritative stance he was only just learning, stood blocking the cell door and said Hold on now, hold on, we still have to issue the paperwork. The buzzmen glanced at him and took no notice, as tho he were a frail little boy talking to his stuffed animals. They went back to what they were doing and he said No! I said no! We haven't contacted his next of kin! He'd raised his voice but beneath the words could be heard the start of a sob. This time, for the first time, the buzzmen stared at him with faces that said The fuck does this little shit think he's doing? and put the body down – a body they knew was not the kind of body you take to the family – and stood clenching and unclenching fists, reconciled to a whole other asskicking, but suddenly it was not their fists but someone else's hand he felt on his shoulder, and he turned and saw the biggest bastard in the barrio, the one who'd gotten him this gig, who said: Thanks for everything, counselor, we'll take it from here. And the big bastard smiled at him like a brother.

He thought of the man's look, which he'd never gotten out of his head; of what he himself looked like in the other man's eyes; of the fact that some sort of agreement had been reached in that final moment, when he shook his head mechanically side to side, more an entreaty than an order.

The barrio bastard, who at the time had a whole nose and both lungs, gestured affably to the buzzmen to take the body out as tho waving them into his house, then faced him and said it: Trust me, kid, I got your back.

And he decided not to keep shaking his head, not to keep blocking their way with his own body to prevent them from removing the other, not to say a word. And that was the precise instant when he first felt the presence of the black dog, who would never again leave him, who might sometimes slip out of sight, but would always be there.

He learned to live with the cur, at times even to conjure him. Yes, something inside him broke, but that's what made it possible to go places and make decisions he could never have stomached on his own. His black dog was a dark mass that allowed him to do certain things, to not feel certain things, he was physical, as real as a bone you don't know you have until it's almost jutting through your skin.

The Redeemer recalled all of this and brought his face up close to Dolphin's and said again, nearly touching his nose, Fraid you can't do that.

Dolphin pulled back a bit and eyed him with scorn.

Why's that? Because you got your little door locked?

So the Redeemer pulled out his key, slipped it in the lock, turned it, opened the door and stood aside.

Still can't do that.

Dolphin, face still full of scorn, said You'd drown in a glass of water, and placed a hand on the doorjamb, but at that moment the Unruly grabbed him by one wrist.

The man said no.

Dolphin turned to her in utter astonishment. There had to be some mistake.

We can talk later, now stop fucking around and behave.

But jerking his arm, the Unruly spun him around.

No. It's time for you to grit your teeth and swallow.

Dolphin was about to say something but she squeezed his wrist a little tighter.

Enough. Don't be stupid.

Dolphin glanced down at the arm cuffed by his own daughter's hand for a few seconds, perhaps listening to himself wheeze, then nodded as tho he'd been the one who decided to go. He cast the Redeemer a casual sidelong glance by way of farewell and ambled slowly toward the entrance.

At the door he turned for a moment and said One of these days something terrible is going to happen.

And left.

That it might, the Redeemer thought, But no way am I letting you in to despoil a dead body.

Before going back inside Three Times Blonde's he went to the Big House door to make sure it was actually locked but first stepped out on the street. Still an overcast morning, he thought. Afternoon, he corrected himself. We're still alone, not even anyone to offer wrong directions. And then he thought he heard a muffled sound to his left, but didn't bother to turn and look to see what it was, since nothing but the lingering trace of silent complaint seemed possible in that bleak and stricken city. Or because his black dog wasn't there to remind him that anything was possible. And he felt a cold wooden crack! on his cranium and saw the sidewalk rush up at his face and then took the tip of a shoe to his ribs and then to his cheekbone and a heel rammed repeatedly into his ear. It hurt like a bitch, he had to start hitting back, beat the motherloving life out of someone, he said to himself, and still hoped he might as he clamped onto a fist that he used to raise himself, but then came another blow and something in him disconnected, like he'd been detached from a rock and was falling through an open pit, dark and icy, a pit with no walls and no end.

5

He awoke and saw the overcast sky falling onto his eyes. It felt as tho the darkness had gone on for hours, but it couldn't have been more than a few minutes, since there was the Neeyanderthal, who'd said on the phone he was on his way over.

He'd dreamed. Or more than dreams he'd seen snapshots of a devious Egyptian bug clamping gleefully onto his neck.

It looked like a block party, with all the people there outside the Big House: a white-shirted, blue-trousered buzz-cut heap of a man lay sprawled a few inches away; the Neeyanderthal stood effortlessly restraining Three Times Blonde's slicked-back jack on the ground; and Three Times Blonde herself was peering from the half-open door of the Big House, her face fearful but also sort of fascinated.

No, really, it's all over, here, let me help you up, Neeyan was saying to the guy. Let me give you a hand.

The little jack made as if to accept the offer and the Neeyanderthal pushed him back down, all the force of his open hand on the man's face.

Don't raise your hand to me, you little shit.

And he laughed and said No no, sorry brother, I was being a dick, here, get up, we'll talk.

Little slick conched himself into his tiny shell of a world there on the sidewalk and the Neeyanderthal smacked him again.

Answer when you're spoken to.

Enough, Neeyan, the Redeemer said from his own piece of sidewalk. It's not like the little prick doesn't have motive.

We're just having a chat, the Neeyanderthal replied.

The Redeemer himself had been shitkicked in seconds, so who knows how the Neeyanderthal had managed to take the two of them down with no help from anyone. Maybe he should feel guilty for mixing his friend up in fights that weren't even his, but some time ago he'd decided that if the man wanted to kill himself anyway, why worry about it. I am one lowly sonofabitch, he thought.

From the corner of his eye he glimpsed something stirring, but by the time he turned to look, the heap that had accompanied little slick was already on his feet and wielding a blade with the resolve of a man who doesn't carry it for effect. He lunged at the Neeyanderthal, who for a split second made no move, his face saying Whatever shall be shall be – like this was some sort of favor – and when the tip of the blade was almost to his stomach he snatched the heap's wrist with one hand and twisted, but the rest of the body failed to turn at the same speed and you could clearly hear how his wrist went snap before the whole heap of him slammed against the sidewalk.

The Neeyanderthal looked happy, as tho just bathed, or even born.

Maybe it's not that he wants to die, the Redeemer thought, but that what he wants is not to stumble.

Damn, Neeyan, he said, We ought to get you on TV.

Nah, the Neeyanderthal replied. No point being famous; then they'd just say I never existed.

The Redeemer got to his feet and said to the two bruisers: Go.

The heap crawled a few feet, then pulled himself up and quickly scampered to the corner. Little slick sat still in his own world, exploring the insides of his arms. Finally he stood and went to the Big House door. On seeing him Three Times Blonde slammed it shut.

You think you're coming in here? Look at you!

What?

There's an epidemic out there and you got nothing on. I bet you're already sick.

I had a mask on, whined her beau. But that bastard smacked it off.

There ensued a brief silence. Three Times Blonde cracked the door for a sec and stared him in the eye.

That's what they all say, she said.

And closed it again.

The minute Not-so-slick took his leave, Vicky turned up. She saw them all in the distance, standing before the Big House, and surveyed the terrain on approach. Before saying a word she followed him with her eyes, then looked at the Neeyanderthal, then at the bloody splash-up on the sidewalk, and finally at the Redeemer.

Want me to tell you about it? asked the Neeyanderthal.

Vicky scanned the scene again with something like a surplus of sadness and began to examine the Redeemer, feeling his neck, looking at his eyes, the cut above one brow, the split lip. The Redeemer's ribs were still shaking but she didn't think they were broken.

Open your mouth, Vicky said. The Redeemer opened his mouth and Vicky prodded a canine with one finger.

This tooth's done for, she said. But the rest of the prick'll survive.

One more thing, said the Redeemer: Check and see if I have anything here.

He pointed to his neck. Vicky tilted his head a bit and looked. She stood back, looked at him again.

What do you think you have there?

You see a welt?

Vicky looked again.

I see something, but it could be a heel mark. If you were going to die you'd feel awful by now. That's what I've been seeing at the hospital. Things don't usually escalate this quick, but sometimes these fuckers can remember if they've been in a certain place before, and that makes them really hard to stop. Things do more damage the second time around.

If it was merely a question of feeling awful, the Redeemer was infected as shit, but for now he felt the contamination was contained to the places he'd been kicked.

Let's go look at Baby Girl, he said.

I'm staying here, the Neeyanderthal said. More fun.

He opened the door and at that moment a call came in. Vicky went ahead.

Friend – it was the Mennonite – all good over there?

All good, why?

Just got word the Las Pericas place is on fire.

What the . . . ? he thought. How would the Mennonite even know to associate Las Pericas with Dolphin?

The place is on fire . . . And you're telling me the Castros aren't behind it, the Redeemer said.

I'm saying the Castros aren't behind it, the Mennonite replied. Been here the whole time. All the father wants is his daughter back, and at a time like this his boys aren't about to do anything without his say-so.

Got it. All good here. Anything happens I'll give you a call.

They hung up. It was time to try Gustavo again. He dialed and found him in. Come on over, the man said.

He walked into the Big House. Inside his apartment, Vicky was washing one of Baby Girl's arms with a wet rag. Some bodies need to be assessed; this one needed to be dressed.

I'm leaving you here with her, he said. Won't be long.

Vicky nodded without turning to look, and the Redeemer walked out.

Be right back, he said to the Neeyanderthal.

Where you off to?

Going to see Gustavo, but I need you to stay here.

Bet you'll smoke a blunt, the Neeyanderthal said.

The Redeemer got into the Bug and drove off. On the way to Gustavo's he stopped a second in front of Las Pericas. The facade was still standing but the flames inside the place were devouring it all and already licking at the windows. No firemen or onlookers to distract the fire.

He got to Gustavo's. His was not a hood but a neighborhood, a bit better painted but equally as deserted as where the Redeemer lived. He got out, knocked and after a few seconds a girl came to the door. She couldn't have been more than fifteen or sixteen, and was pregnant. Come in, she said quietly, and turned.

The floors, walls, furniture, doorknobs, all of it possessed a soap-scrubbed shine, less a clean house than some sort of mausoleum holding the outside world at bay. Gustavo was sitting in an armchair in the living room. You could tell he'd just come from court because he'd yet to take off his coat and tie. The Redeemer hadn't laid eyes on him for a couple years. The man was still in shape, but his chin-sag and dark-circled eyes said he'd seen the better side of sixty some time ago. The girl handed the Redeemer a facemask. She looked sleep-deprived or anemic.

Mamacita, bring the attorney here a beer, Gustavo said.

On his way in, the Redeemer had not noticed that behind her was a boy with a baby-walker. Something was the matter with him. He was smiling and moving his legs but not making much progress, his eyes unfocused.

So, you working too?

Fraid so.

At the foot of the sofa sat a metal pail of marijuana. Gustavo took out a sheet of rice paper, then another, and licked the length of both to make one long sheet. He rolled a leisurely spliff as fat as a churro and when he saw the Redeemer eyeing it said I'm not giving you any; feel free to roll your own.

And toed the pail over to him.

I'm good, said the Redeemer.

So. How can I be of service?

The Las Pericas place.

What about it?

It's on fire.

Gustavo arched his eyebrows and opened his eyes wide but didn't release the tank of smoke he'd sucked into his lungs. He held it a few more seconds and then, after exhaling, said: God's will that was, I'm surprised it didn't happen sooner.

Why?

Had it coming, that's why.

Gustavo took another big hit of his spliff and waited, making the Redeemer work for it.

What happened?

They aren't two families is what happened, he replied: They're one, or almost, his voice tight with smoke. The two fathers have the same father. That's what happened.

And he expelled the smoke.

The Castros' father married on the up-and-up, but one day he got the hots for this girl in the neighborhood, took off with her and started another family. All well and good so far, right? Just the way it is. But then the old fucker went and died, fifteen years or so after he and his second woman had been living together. And that's when this all started up.

The girl came in with a beer for the Redeemer and Gustavo said Wait.

He stroked her ass and blew her a big smacking kiss. The girl remained motionless.

You'd never met my wife, had you? She's a saint. Okay, mamacita, now run and make me one of those highballs you're so good at.

The girl left.

Gustavo – this Gustavo – could never have existed in another age. For the first time in the history of humankind, legions of men his age could fuck like they were decades younger. The things they'll never discover, these old men who can still get it up, thought the Redeemer. As if there's nothing to be learned from defeat.

We live in extraordinary times, Gustavo said. People nowadays are aware of so much stuff going on in the world that they can handpick their memories. Didn't used to be like that, people used to live in whatever world their parents had left them. Some still do, like this gang – holding on and holding on.

To what?

The body. The day of the wake, the other family – the first one – came out, just to pay their respects and say their goodbyes. The widows greeted each another, the boys ignored each other – each family had a teenager almost the same age, see – and that was it. But when the Castros found out they were going to bury him who-knows-where, well that was the fuckin end of good form. Turns out the Fonsecas belong to some sort of sect, call themselves Christians but don't belong to the church.

It's always the other guy's religion that's a sect, isn't it? the Redeemer asked, unwisely, since he knew it was best to let people talk without rankling. Gustavo gave him a quick look like he'd had food thrown in his face, took another toke and continued.

After that, no surprises: widow number one asked them nicely not to bury him there, then demanded they not bury him there, but since the other one kept saying no no no, widow one said she wasn't going to let them do that, she wasn't the legitimate wife for nothing, they'd see. Off she went, lawyered up, and came back. The Fonseca widow said they better not think they were going to take the body, and the lawyers brought some cops along.

Did they get it?

Well sure – corpse was in their name. Son of the second family didn't even get his dad's last name, supposedly to avoid complications. Ha! So they kicked up a fuss, there was back-and-forthing, there were threats, but what I remember best is that kid, Dolphin. Back then he wasn't called that. The way he clenched his fists and stared at the coffin as they carried it out, his eyes little slits full of rage.

Gustavo leaned forward to check if his drink was on the way but couldn't see the kitchen from where he sat. The Redeemer could, tho, and saw the girl uncorking a bottle of brandy.

Thing is, he hadn't left a will, Gustavo continued, And the house where he and his second lady lived was in both their names, but the house they were about to move to was only in his.

Las Pericas.

Right. And ever since then there've been legal proceedings to see who gets to keep it, tho I know Dolphin has a key and pokes his head in, time to time. Might just be a good thing it's burning down. Nobody likes to share money, but it's easier than sharing a fistful of ashes.

They'd had no Redeemer to lend them a hand, the Redeemer thought.

Well now there's fewer to share them between, but more ashes to go around.

Eh?

Dolphin's son died, and so did the Castros' daughter. And each family has the other one's corpse.

For a second Gustavo's eyes popped out of their sockets.

Shoot-out?

Now the Redeemer was the one to enjoy letting the information steep a few seconds, as he took a sip of his beer.

Coincidence.

Gustavo narrowed his eyes.

Those things just don't happen, he said.

He was tempted to smoke a joint but decided not to ask. It was time to go. He glanced toward the kitchen to say goodbye to the girl and saw her with one hand inside Gustavo's glass, staring fixedly at the wall while she fingered the ice, as if cleaning it. The scene had the innocence of all unsettling things that take place in silence.

He bought more flowers on his way back and stopped to watch a madman who used to bounce around among the cars until one of them would whack him to the curb. Now, with no traffic, he was walking on the sidewalk.

What you doing? he asked. But the madman only stared as tho the question was idiotic.

He arranged with the Mennonite to make the trade on the corner closest to the Big House. With the way the city was, better to do it quick and out in the open than try to find some other spot. He called Dolphin, too, and told him it was time, that he should head over, but to let him do his job.

The Neeyanderthal had gone inside and was sitting in his apartment having coffee with Vicky, next to the bed where Baby Girl lay. The water must've come back on.

They're on the way, he said. Look alive, Neeyan, and let me know when they get here.

The Neeyanderthal finished his coffee and left. The Redeemer took his seat.

I won't mix you up in this shit again, he told Vicky.

At least this time it feels like it matters, she replied.

They said nothing more. Everything was so quiet you could hear Baby Girl's silence, as tho she'd absorbed every sound in the room. It was hard and yet formless, that silence. How to describe what isn't there? What name can you give to something that doesn't exist yet exists for that reason precisely? Kings of the kingpins, those who had invented the zero, he thought, had given it a name and even slipped it into a line of numbers, as tho it could stay put, obedient. But once in a while, like at that moment, there before Baby Girl, zero rose up and swallowed everything.

They're on the corner, the Neeyanderthal shouted from out front.

I'll get Neeyan so he can help you carry Baby Girl, Vicky said.

No no no, that cat's too rough, he might hurt her.

Vicky stood and stared, in astonishment or perplexity, or maybe even admiration.

In that case I'll help.

They got close to the bed and he slid one arm under Baby Girl's back and the other beneath her knees while Vicky cradled her head. He attempted to lift her but the pain in his ribs made him put the body back down. Fuckit, he said. He tried again and again doubled over, fuckit, and he didn't know why but knew he was about to cry.

Squat down, Vicky said. Then stand up slowly and I'll take her back too.

They did that, and as soon as he sensed that he held all her weight he stood as fast as he could.

Vicky placed Baby Girl's arms carefully on top of her body and then positioned her head like she was curled up against the Redeemer's chest.

Let's go, he said.

Vicky opened one door then ran and opened the next, as he followed in a juddering stumble of painful steps; Motherfucker, he said to each bruise and then to his whole body, Fuck you fuckin motherfucker; and then to her body: Don't you go and fall on me, Baby Girl, don't you fuckin even think about falling.

It was dark out now, but in addition to that there was something different in the atmosphere, the temperature had dropped and the air had finally come unstuck; it wasn't exactly windy but you could tell wind was on the cards. And the sky was clear and there was light coming from below.

You want me to help you? asked the Neeyanderthal, seeing him on the verge of collapse.

No.

Then carry her properly, this ain't luggage you're delivering.

I know that.

He saw Dolphin's truck round one corner. He and the Unruly were alone. They got out and the Neeyanderthal approached to check for gats or shanks or other instruments of slaughter.

The Redeemer straightened up tall and strode to the other corner, where the towering silhouette of the Mennonite, the fidgety shapes of the Castro kids and the tip of the father's cigarette could be discerned. Behind them a black hearse. Romeo's mother wasn't coming. Sometimes mothers come out to collect their children, other times they stay home no matter what, to make sure their children have a place prepared for them when they get back.

The Mennonite took a few steps forward then stopped and stood before the Redeemer. He looked Baby Girl over carefully.

Any need to inspect her?

None at all. I trust you're delivering Romeo exactly as he was yesterday?

Every inch untouched.

The Mennonite turned and walked back to the corner, circled the hearse and came back, boy in arms. The Neeyanderthal received him, and almost simultaneously the Redeemer delivered Baby Girl to her brothers. Up until that moment the families had been silent, but when the Neeyanderthal got close with Romeo, the Unruly stepped back and started sobbing disconsolately, shrieking with her mouth covered, hands choking back her cries. Trembling, it took her several small steps to make it to her brother tho she wasn't far at all, and then finally she embraced him and cried on his chest. On the other side, the Castro brothers were placing Baby Girl into the hearse and weeping but not allowing themselves to sob. Their father shook his head slowly side to side; then, suddenly, he took a decisive step toward Dolphin, and the Mennonite took another in case he tried anything, but all the man did was point at the hearse, glowing ember at the end of his hand, and open his mouth without finding any words, until finally he said They told me she got sick, that you didn't kill her, and I believe them, but what call was there to go and fuck us over like this? All for what? Fighting over ashes.

They were my ashes, Dolphin said. And when he said it he sounded as if he possessed a strength he no longer did, said it without wheezing, with that lung he'd been missing for years.

The other man waited a few seconds before replying. You're right. But Baby Girl's not to blame for that.

Dolphin had nothing more to say. The other man turned back to the hearse and opened the door to get in.

She never liked being called that, the Unruly shouted after him, and he turned to look. I have a name, that's what she said the day I took her home with me, don't call me Baby Girl. And she told me her name.

The Castro patriarch glanced at her a second then said I know my daughter's name.

And he got into the hearse. Before following him, the Mennonite came over to say goodbye. They bumped fists.

You going back home? The Redeemer asked.

Nah. I don't even know if there's anywhere to go back to.

The Redeemer approached the Unruly and said Give him a call.

She looked at him, uncomprehending.

Your brother-in-law.

The Unruly nodded yes and turned.

The Neeyanderthal accompanied the Fonsecas to their truck and placed Romeo into the box. Since they were going different directions, the families crossed each other once more, but this time no one looked. So many things had been hurled, things written in stone, that the street lay in ruins.

The Redeemer watched the hearse drive away. Who will bury that girl? he wondered. Because it won't be them, those who wept so much and threatened so much, they won't be the ones to dig her grave. When did we stop burying those we love with our own hands? he thought. From people like us, what the hell can we expect?

A cold breeze began, timidly. The Neeyanderthal rubbed his hands together and said What now? You got juice?

No, Neeyan, Vicky said. It's time to go. Each of us will clean our guts our own way.

Okay, the Neeyanderthal replied, and looked the Redeemer up and down. I'd say I hope your way involves getting it on with the neighbor, but shit, state you're in I think you'll keel over before you can say bless my soul.

He gave him a rough pat on the back and said We're outta here.

Vicky came to give him a kiss and, right as she was about to, turned to one side and sneezed into her elbow.

Maybe one day people wouldn't even remember when everyone had started doing it like that, instead of covering their noses with their hands. It takes a serious scare for some gestures to take hold but then they end up like scars that seem to have been there all along. Maybe they themselves would one day be nothing but someone's scar, nameless, no epitaph, just a line on the skin.

Because like everything, this too would pass, and the world would act innocent for a while, until it scared them shitless once more.

The two of them left, and the Redeemer entered the Big House. He tried to remember a good mantra but the only thing that came to mind was Let them burn me and turn me, mark me and merk me – and that wasn't what he wanted.

Three Times Blonde opened the door and the Redeemer walked in.

She took a look at his split lip and stroked the scab on his head.

People are fools, she said. They spend their whole lives getting stuck with pins and act like nothing's wrong, they just leave them there, and then one day they go and scratch someone's eyes out.

The truth is, the Redeemer said, maybe we're damned from the start.

What truth? Three Times Blonde looked at him like he was an idiot. I don't buy that crap, that *Look but don't touch* stuff. Tell me, what truth? Maybe someone out there knows, but it's not me, so I call it like I see it.

And she poked a dieresis into his chest.

The Redeemer placed a hand on her back and ran it all the way down and over the curve of her ass.

Plus, she went on, they said on TV people are getting better now, that they really know what it is and there's no reason to die.

They pressed up against the wall and the Redeemer kissed her a bit of his blood. Suddenly Three Times Blonde cocked her head and said Listen.

A wavering windstorm was blowing outside the Big House. Maybe the clouds are gone, she said, and let go of the Redeemer.

The Redeemer observed her profile, so luscious and tuned-in to the sounds on the street. Talk and cock is all I got, he thought. And sometimes fear.

I'm tired of being cooped up, Three Times Blonde said.

She walked out into the hall and then onto the street and the Redeemer followed, but before he caught up to her at the front door, la Ñora's opened.

Are your visitors gone?

They are, señora, thank you for your discretion.

Young man, said la Ñora. You knew, didn't you?

The Redeemer had known, but he also knew sometimes it was best not to say. So he said nothing.

He got mad and left, la Ñora went on. And I thought I'd never hear from him again, that's the way it is these days, people just disappear, but someone called from the courts, a young lady he told to phone me. I don't know why they're holding him. He says he's black and blue but they've stopped beating him now.

La Ñora paused to allow the Redeemer to intervene and he hoped against hope that she wasn't asking what she seemed to be asking.

I'm going to go get him, la Ñora said. Do you know where the place is?

Fuckit, she was, she was asking. For a moment he considered the possibility of letting the little sonofabitch spend the night in the hoosegow but he couldn't do it. Perhaps Gustavo was right: these days we walk past a body on the street, and we have to stop pretending we can't see it.

Aren't you afraid you might get whatever this is? he asked her.

Me? I don't get anything anymore, not even tired.

Best not to go out, señora, I'll get him and bring him back to you, I just have to do one thing first.

Thank you, young man.

He headed for the door.

Young man, said la Ñora.

The Redeemer turned.

I didn't ask for this.

The Redeemer nodded.

He turned. Be right back, he said to himself. And he opened the Big House door and went out to look at the stars once again.

Dear readers,

We rely on subscriptions from people like you to tell these other stories – the types of stories most publishers consider too risky to take on.

Our subscribers don't just make the books physically happen. They also help us approach booksellers, because we can demonstrate that our books already have readers and fans. And they give us the security to publish in line with our values, which are collaborative, imaginative and 'shamelessly literary'.

All of our subscribers:

- receive a first-edition copy of each of the books they subscribe to
- are thanked by name at the end of our subscriber-supported books
- receive little extras from us by way of thank you, for example: postcards created by our authors

BECOME A SUBSCRIBER, OR GIVE A SUBSCRIPTION TO A FRIEND

Visit andotherstories.org/subscribe to become part of an alternative approach to publishing.

Subscriptions are:
£20 for two books per year
£35 for four books per year
£50 for six books per year

OTHER WAYS TO GET INVOLVED

If you'd like to know about upcoming events and reading groups (our foreign-language reading groups help us choose books to publish, for example) you can:

- join the mailing list at: andotherstories.org/join-us
- follow us on Twitter: @andothertweets
- join us on Facebook: facebook.com/AndOtherStoriesBooks
- follow our blog: Ampersand

This book was made possible thanks to the support of:

Aaron McEnery · Abigail Dawson · Abigail Miller · Ada Gokay · Adam Butler · Adam Lenson · Aino Efraimsson · Ajay Sharma · Alan Ramsey · Alana Marquis-Farncombe · Alannah Hopkin · Alasdair Thomson · Alastair Maude · Alastair Laing · Alastair Gillespie · Alastair Dickson · Alex Martin · Alex Ramsey · Alex Sutcliffe · Alex Gregory · Alexandra Citron · Alexandra de Verseg-Roesch · Ali Smith · Ali Conway · Alice Nightingale · Alison Lock · Alison Hughes · Alison Layland · Allison Graham · Allyson Dowling · Alyse Ceirante · Amanda Dalton · Amanda · Amanda DeMarco · Amelia Ashton · Amelia Dowe · Amine Hamadache · Andrew Lees · Andrew McCallum · Andrew McAlpine · Andrew Kerr-Jarrett · Andrew Rego · Andrew McCafferty · Andrew Marston · Andy Madeley · Angela Everitt · Angela Creed · Angus Walker · Anna Vinegrad · Anna Milsom · Anna Britten · Anna-Karin Palm · Annalisa Quaini · Annalise Pippard · Anne Marsella · Anne Carus · Anne Claire Le Reste · Anne Marie Jackson · Annie McDermott · Anonymous · Anonymous · Anonymous · Anthony Carrick · Anthony Quinn · Antonia Lloyd-Jones · Antonio de Swift · Antony Pearce · Aoife Boyd · Archie Davies · Arline Dillman · Asako Serizawa · Asher Norris · Audrey Mash · Ayca Turkoglu · Barbara Devlin · Barbara Anderson · Barbara Robinson · Barbara Mellor · Barbara Adair · Barry Hall · Barry John Fletcher · Bartolomiej Tyszka · Belinda Farrell · Ben Schofield · Ben Thornton · Benjamin Morris · Benjamin Judge · Bernard Devaney · Beth Mcintosh · Bianca Winter · Bianca Jackson · Bob Richmond-Watson · Brendan McIntyre · Briallen Hopper · Brigita Ptackova · Bruno Angelucci · Calum Colley · Candida Lacey · Carl Emery · Carole Hogan · Caroline Smith · Caroline Perry · Cassidy Hughes · Catherine Taylor · Catrin Ashton · Cecilia Rossi & Iain Robinson · Cecily Maude · Charles Lambert · Charlotte Holtam · Charlotte Whittle · Charlotte Ryland · Charlotte Murrie & Stephen Charles · Chia Foon Yeow · China Miéville · Chloe Schwartz · Chris Holmes · Chris Stevenson · Chris Day · Chris Gribble · Chris Elcock · Christine Carlisle · Christine Luker · Christopher Jackson · Christopher Terry · Christopher Allen · Ciara Ní Riain · Claire Williams · Clarissa Botsford · Claudio Guerri · Clifford Posner · Clive Bellingham · Clodie Vasli · Colin Matthews · Colin Burrow · Courtney Lilly · Craig Barney · Dan Pope · Daniel Kennedy · Daniel Gillespie · Daniel Rice · Daniel Coxon · Daniel Arnold · Daniel Venn · Daniel Lipscombe · Daniel Gallimore · Daniel Carpenter · Daniel Hahn · Daniela Steierberg · Dave Young · Davi Rocha · David Smith · David Gould · David Johnstone · David Shriver · David Higgins · David Johnson-Davies · David Hedges · David Roberts · David Hebblethwaite · Deborah Jacob · Deborah Bygrave · Denise Jones · Dermot McAleese · Dianna Campbell · Dimitris Melicertes · Dominique Brocard · Duncan Ranslem · Duncan Marks · Ed Owles · Elaine Rassaby · Eleanor Maier · Elie Howe · Eliza O'Toole · Elizabeth Bryer · Elizabeth Heighway · Elsbeth Julie Watering · Emily McLean-Inglis · Emily Gray · Emily Diamand · Emily Williams · Emily Taylor · Emily Jeremiah · Emily Yaewon Lee & Gregory Limpens · Emma Turesson · Emma Perry · Emma Bielecki · Emma Timpany · Emma Teale · Emma Yearwood · Emma Louise Grove · Eric E Rubeo · Erin Louttit · Eva Tobler-Zumstein · Ewan Tant · Fawzia Kane · Finbarr Farragher · Finnuala Butler · Fiona Marquis · Fiona Graham · Fiona Malby · Fiona Quinn · Fran Sanderson · Frances Hazelton · Francis Taylor · Francisco

Vilhena · Friederike Knabe · Gabrielle Crockatt · Gabrielle Turner · Gavin Collins · Gawain Espley · Genevra Richardson · Genia Ogrenchuk · Geoff Thrower · Geoffrey Cohen · Geoffrey Urland · George Wilkinson · George Savona · George McCaig · George Quentin Baker · George Sandison & Daniela Laterza · Georgia Mill · Georgia Panteli · Gerard Mehigan · Gerry Craddock · Gill Ord · Gill Boag-Munroe · Gina Dark · Gordon Cameron · Graham R Foster · Gregory Conti · Guy Haslam · Hannah Jones · Hannah Perrett · Hans Lazda · Harriet Mossop · Heather Fielding · Helen Bailey · Helen Wormald · Helen Jones · Helen Poulsen · Helen Asquith · Helen Weir · Helen Collins · Helen Brady · Helene Walters-Steinberg · Henriette Heise · Henrike Laehnemann · Henry Wall · Ian Holding · Ian Kirkwood · Ian McMillan · Ignês Sodré · Ingrid Olsen · Irene Mansfield · Isabella Weibrecht · Isabella Garment · Isobel Dixon · Isobel Staniland · Jack McNamara · Jack Brown · Jacqueline Taylor · Jacqueline Haskell · Jacqueline Lademann · James Wilper · James Tierney · James Scudamore · James Kinsley · James Warner · James Beck · James Attlee · James Portlock · James Cubbon · Jamie Walsh · Jane Keeley · Jane Woollard · Jane Whiteley · Janet Sarbanes · Janet Mullarney · Janette Ryan · Jasmine Gideon · JC Sutcliffe · Jean-Jacques Regouffre · Jeff Collins · Jen Hamilton-Emery · Jennifer O'Brien · Jennifer Humbert · Jennifer Hearn · Jennifer Higgins · Jennifer Hurstfield · Jenny Newton · Jeremy Faulk · Jeremy Weinstock · Jess Conway · Jess Howard-Armitage · Jessica Hopkins · Jessica Schouela · Jethro Soutar · Jillian Jones · Jim Boucherat · Jo Harding · Joanna Luloff · Joanna Flower · Joel Love · Johan Forsell · Johanna Eliasson · Johannes Georg Zipp · John Steigerwald · John Down · John Royley · John Conway · John Hodgson · John Griffiths · John Gent · John Kelly · Jon Riches · Jon Lindsay Miles · Jonathan Watkiss · Joseph Cooney · Joshua Davis · JP Sanders · Judith Blair · Julia Rochester · Julia Thum · Julian Lomas · Julian Duplain · Julie Van Pelt · Julie Gibson · Juliet Swann · Kaarina Hollo · Kapka Kassabova · Karen Davison · Katarina Trodden · Kate Cooper · Kate Beswick · Kate Gardner · Kate Griffin · Katharina Liehr · Katharine Nurse · Katharine Freeman · Katharine Robbins · Katherine Green · Katherine Sotejeff-Wilson · Katherine Skala · Katherine El-Salahi · Kathryn Edwards · Kathryn Bogdanowitsch-Johnston · Kathryn Lewis · Katie Brown · Katrina Thomas · Keith Walker · Kent McKernan · Kevin Winter · Kiera Vaclavik · Kimberli Drain · KL Ee · Kristin Djuve · Lana Selby · Lara Touitou · Laura Lea · Laura Batatota · Laura Drew · Lauren Ellemore · Lauren McCormick · Laurence Laluyaux · Leanne Bass · Leigh Vorhies · Leonie Schwab · Leri Price · Lesley Watters · Lesley Lawn · Lesley Taylor · Leslie Rose · Linda Walz · Lindsay Brammer · Lindsey Stuart · Lindsey Ford · Linnea Frank · Liz Wilding · Liz Ketch · Liz Clifford · Lizzie Broadbent · Loretta Platts · Lorna Bleach · Louise Bongiovanni · Luc Verstraete · Lucia Rotheray · Lucy Webster · Lucy Caldwell · Luke Healey · Lynn Schneider · Lynn Martin · M Manfre · Madeleine Kleinwort · Maeve Lambe · Maggie Livesey · Maggie Peel · Mandy Wight · Mandy Boles · Margaret Begg · Margaret Irish · Margaret Jull Costa · Maria Cotera · Maria Pelletta · Marina Castledine · Mark Waters · Mark Lumley · Mark Ainsbury · Marlene Adkins · Martha Gifford · Martha Nicholson · Martin Brampton · Martin Price · Mary Wang · Mary Nash · Mathias Enard · Matt & Owen Davies · Matthew Geden · Matthew Thomas · Matthew Smith · Matthew O'Dwyer · Matthew Francis · Maureen McDermott · Meaghan Delahunt ·

Megan Wittling · Melissa Beck · Melissa Quignon-Finch · Melissa da Silveira Serpa · Melvin Davis · Merima Jahic · Michael Holtmann · Michael Ward · Michael Aguilar · Michael Moran · Michael Johnston · Michelle Bailat-Jones · Michelle Roberts · Michelle Dyrness · Milo Waterfield · Miranda Persaud · Miranda Petruska · Mitchell Albert · Molly Ashby · Monika Olsen · Morgan Lyons · Najiba · Nan Haberman · Naomi Kruger · Nasser Hashmi · Natalie Smith · Nathan Rostron · Neil Griffiths · Neil Pretty · Nia Emlyn-Jones · Nick Rombes · Nick Sidwell · Nick Chapman · Nick James · Nick Nelson & Rachel Eley · Nicola Hart · Nienke Pruiksma · Nina Alexandersen · Nina Power · Nuala Watt · Octavia Kingsley · Olga Zilberbourg · Olivia Payne · Pamela Ritchie · Pat Morgan · Pat Crowe · Patricia Appleyard · Patrick Owen · Paul Robinson · Paul Griffiths · Paul Munday · Paul Bailey · Paul Brand · Paul Jones · Paul Gamble · Paul Myatt · Paul C Daw · Paul M Cray · Paula Edwards · Paula Ely · Penelope Hewett Brown · Peter McCambridge · Peter Vos · Peter Rowland · Philip Warren · Phillip Canning · Phyllis Reeve · Piet Van Bockstal · PJ Abbott · PM Goodman · Poppy Collinson · PRAH Recordings · R & AS Bromley · Rachael Williams · Rachael MacFarlane · Rachel Matheson · Rachel Carter · Rachel Lasserson · Rachel Kennedy · Rachel Van Riel · Rachel Watkins · Read MAW Books · Rebecca Carter · Rebecca Braun · Rebecca Rosenthal · Rebecca Moss · Rhiannon Armstrong · Richard Priest · Richard Steward · Richard Ross · Richard Major · Richard Ellis · Richard Soundy · Richard Martin · Richard Jackson · Richard Hoey & Helen Crump · Rishi Dastidar · Rob Jefferson-Brown · Robert Gillett · Robin Taylor · Robin Patterson · Roderick Lauder · Ros Schwartz · Rosalia Rodriguez-Garcia · Rose Skelton · Rosie Pinhorn · Roz Simpson · Rupert Walz · Ruth Diver · SJ Bradley · SJ Naudé · Sabine Griffiths · Sacha Craddock · Sally Baker · Sam Cunningham · Sam Gordon · Sam Ruddock · Samantha Smith · Samantha Sabbarton-Wright · Samantha Sawers · Sandra Hall · Sandra de Monte · Sara C Hancock · Sarah Benson · Sarah Lippek · Sarah Pybus · Sarah Salmon · Sarah Butler · Sean Malone · Sean McGivern · Seini O'Connor · Sergio Gutierrez Negron · Sheridan Marshall · Shirley Harwood · Simon James · Simon Armstrong · Simone Van Dop & Tom Rutter · Simone O'Donovan · Siobhan Jones · Sioned Puw Rowlands · Siriol Hugh-Jones · SJ Nevin · Sjón · Sonia Overall · Sonia McLintock · Sophia Wickham · Stefanie May IV · Steph Morris · Stephanie Brada · Stephen Walker · Stephen Karakassidis · Stephen Pearsall · Stephen Bass · Stephen H Oakey · Steven Norton · Steven Reid · Sue & Ed Aldred · Sue Eaglen & Colin Crewdson · Susan Higson · Susan Lea · Susan Tomaselli · Susie Roberson · Suzanne Ross · Swannee Welsh · Sylvie Zannier-Betts · Tammi Owens · Tammy Harman · Tammy Watchorn · Tania Hershman · Tara Cheesman · Terry Kurgan · Thami Fahmy · The Rookery in the Bookery · Thea Bradbury · Thees Spreckelsen · Thomas Mitchell · Thomas Bell · Thomas Fritz · Thomas JD Gray · Tien Do · Tim Jackson · Tim Theroux · Tim Warren · Timothy Harris · Tina Andrews · Tina Rotherham-Winqvist · Todd Greenwood · Tom Franklin · Tom Mandall · Tom Darby · Tom Bowden · Tony Bastow · Tony & Joy Molyneaux · Torna Russell-Hills · Tracy Heuring · Tracy Northup · Trevor Wald · Trevor Lewis · UA Phillips · Val Challen · Vanessa Jackson · Vanessa Nolan · Vasco Dones · Veronica Cockburn · Victoria Anderson · Victoria Adams · Victoria Walker · Visaly Muthusamy · Wendy Langridge · Wenna Price · Will Huxter · William Powell · William G Dennehy · Zac Palmer · Zoë Brasier

Current & Upcoming Books

01
Juan Pablo Villalobos, *Down the Rabbit Hole*
translated from the Spanish by Rosalind Harvey

02
Clemens Meyer, *All the Lights*
translated from the German by Katy Derbyshire

03
Deborah Levy, *Swimming Home*

04
Iosi Havilio, *Open Door*
translated from the Spanish by Beth Fowler

05
Oleg Zaionchkovsky, *Happiness is Possible*
translated from the Russian by Andrew Bromfield

06
Carlos Gamerro, *The Islands*
translated from the Spanish by Ian Barnett

07
Christoph Simon, *Zbinden's Progress*
translated from the German by Donal McLaughlin

08
Helen DeWitt, *Lightning Rods*

09
Deborah Levy, *Black Vodka: ten stories*

10

Oleg Pavlov, *Captain of the Steppe*
translated from the Russian by Ian Appleby

11

Rodrigo de Souza Leão, *All Dogs are Blue*
translated from the Portuguese by Zoë Perry & Stefan Tobler

12

Juan Pablo Villalobos, *Quesadillas*
translated from the Spanish by Rosalind Harvey

13

Iosi Havilio, *Paradises*
translated from the Spanish by Beth Fowler

14

Ivan Vladislavić, *Double Negative*

15

Benjamin Lytal, *A Map of Tulsa*

16

Ivan Vladislavić, *The Restless Supermarket*

17

Elvira Dones, *Sworn Virgin*
translated from the Italian by Clarissa Botsford

18

Oleg Pavlov, *The Matiushin Case*
translated from the Russian by Andrew Bromfield

19

Paulo Scott, *Nowhere People*
translated from the Portuguese by Daniel Hahn

20

Deborah Levy, *An Amorous Discourse in the Suburbs of Hell*

21

Juan Tomás Ávila Laurel, *By Night the Mountain Burns*
translated from the Spanish by Jethro Soutar

22

SJ Naudé, *The Alphabet of Birds*
translated from the Afrikaans by the author

23

Niyati Keni, *Esperanza Street*

24

Yuri Herrera, *Signs Preceding the End of the World*
translated from the Spanish by Lisa Dillman

25

Carlos Gamerro, *The Adventure of the Busts of Eva Perón*
translated from the Spanish by Ian Barnett

26

Anne Cuneo, *Tregian's Ground*
translated from the French by Roland Glasser
and Louise Rogers Lalaurie

27

Angela Readman, *Don't Try This at Home*

28

Ivan Vladislavić, *101 Detectives*

29

Oleg Pavlov, *Requiem for a Soldier*
translated from the Russian by Anna Gunin

30

Haroldo Conti, *Southeaster*
translated from the Spanish by Jon Lindsay Miles

31

Ivan Vladislavić, *The Folly*

32

Susana Moreira Marques, *Now and at the Hour of Our Death*
translated from the Portuguese by Julia Sanches

33

Lina Wolff, *Bret Easton Ellis and the Other Dogs*
translated from the Swedish by Frank Perry

34

Anakana Schofield, *Martin John*

35

Joanna Walsh, *Vertigo*

36

Wolfgang Bauer, *Crossing the Sea*
translated from the German by Sarah Pybus
with photographs by Stanislav Krupař

37

Various, *Lunatics, Lovers and Poets: Twelve Stories after Cervantes and Shakespeare*

38

Yuri Herrera, *The Transmigration of Bodies*
translated from the Spanish by Lisa Dillman

39

César Aira, *The Seamstress and the Wind*
translated from the Spanish by Rosalie Knecht

40

Juan Pablo Villalobos, *I'll Sell You a Dog*
translated from the Spanish by Rosalind Harvey

41

Enrique Vila-Matas, *Vampire in Love*
translated from the Spanish by Margaret Jull Costa

42

Emmanuelle Pagano, *Trysting*
translated from the French by Jennifer Higgins and Sophie Lewis

43

Arno Geiger, *The Old King in his Exile*
translated from the German by Stefan Tobler

Born in Actopan, Mexico, in 1970, **Yuri Herrera** studied Politics in Mexico, Creative Writing in El Paso and took his PhD in literature at Berkeley. His first novel to appear in English, *Signs Preceding the End of the World*, was published to great critical acclaim in 2015 and included in many Best-of-Year lists, including *The Guardian*'s Best Fiction and NBC News's Ten Great Latino Books. He is currently teaching at the University of Tulane, in New Orleans.

Lisa Dillman teaches in the Department of Spanish and Portuguese at Emory University in Atlanta, Georgia. She has translated a number of Spanish and Latin American writers. Some of her recent translations include *Rain Over Madrid*; *August, October*; and *Death of a Horse*, by Andrés Barba, and *Signs Preceding the End of the World* by Yuri Herrera.